LUNGER

T0244309

LUNGER

THE DOC HOLLIDAY STORY

A Novel

PAUL COLT

THORNDIKE PRESS
A part of Gale, a Cengage Company

GALE
A Cengage Company

Copyright © 2023 by Paul Colt.
Thorndike Press, a part of Gale, a Cengage Company.

LIBRARY OF CONGRESS CIP DATA ON FILE.
CATALOGUING IN PUBLICATION FOR THIS BOOK
IS AVAILABLE FROM THE LIBRARY OF CONGRESS.

ISBN-13: 978-1-4205-1605-0 (softcover alk. paper)

Published in 2024 by arrangement with Roan & Weatherford Publishing Associates.

Printed in the USA
2 3 4 5 6   28 27 26 25 24

This book is dedicated to an editor more than a few western writers owe a debt of gratitude, this one included. I didn't know how fortunate I was when Hazel Rumney got the assignment to edit the first book I sold to a major print publisher. I do now. You hear stories about authors and editors knocking heads from time to time. Not so with Hazel. She was my partner on every book until this one. We never had a creative disagreement because I knew the book would be right when Hazel said so. I always thought I might have a chance to thank her publicly one day. She went off to a well-deserved retirement before I got the opportunity, so I guess this dedication will have to do. Hazel deserves more than a little credit and much appreciation for most everything that made it into print with my name on it. This little thank you is long overdue. So, this one's for you Hazel. I hope you approve. Think you might. The word-whittler who wrote it had the best partner and coach a writer could hope for. Some of it must have rubbed off.

JOHN HENRY "DOC" HOLLIDAY (August 14, 1851–November 8, 1887)

PROLOGUE

Hotel Glenwood
Glenwood Springs, Colorado
September 1887

Light gold sepia. Morning. One more. *Cugh, cugh . . . cugh.* So far. It's always sepia. Light seeps through drawn shades. Old gold late afternoon before dark. Gold and dark. Hash strikes on the wall of ma life. What is left of this shriveled husk of a body belongs to John Henry Holliday, better known to notoriety as "Doc." Not by medicine. By dentistry. Forsooth dentistry left me long ago, the profession victim to the ravages of disease. Whiskey, cards, and violence have been ma calling card for much of the time since Ah left Georgia.

Ah glanced around the room. Kate kept me as comfortable as she could. We had our moments, good and bad. The good she held in her heart for me now. The bad? Ah own most of it. Blamed it on the rider of the pale

9

horse followed me all these years. Still, she cares for me beyond ma deserving here at what must come to the last. *Cugh, cugh.* Iron taste. Blood. *Cugh, cugh.* Another stained kerchief. How many has it been? How many . . . has it been? Too many to count.

The door opened. Kate swept into the room with a fresh bottle. "Here, Doc, let me freshen that kerchief for you."

"You are an angel of mercy, Mary Katherine Horony."

"Angel of mercy my ass. Brothels don't produce no angels. Here."

She handed me fresh linen. "Now, if you would, freshen my glass."

"Early to be drinkin' even by your standards, Doc."

"One never knows which glass may be the last. Indulge me."

"I've been indulging you as long as I've known you." She poured.

Ah took a swallow. *Cugh, cugh, cugh.*

"Feel better?"

"Some. How long has it been, love?"

"St. Louis, '72. We were so young."

"Young maybe, but making our way in the world. Dentist and a self-employed lady."

"Self-employed? Soiled dove, you mean, employing my charms. If you're of a nostalgic disposition, at least be honest."

"Seems Ah am reflective this mornin'."

"I remember the first time I laid eyes on you. Big, tall, handsome devil with those lazy blue eyes, hair and moustache neatly trimmed and barbered. A cultured gentleman if there ever was one. Then there was that southern drawl, like butter meltin' on a flapjack. If I hadn't been workin', I'd likely have bedded you for the pleasure of it."

"Ah might blush, had Ah the energy to do so."

"Had plenty of energy in those days."

"Days before the rider of the pale horse came calling. Fresh out of dental college. Figured Ah had the world by the tail."

"As I recall, the tail you had was mine."

"Didn't have much experience with cupidity in those days. Ah do remember you, though. Slip of a girl, pretty as a picture."

"Picture of Mattie."

"Some resemblance, as I recall."

"Likely why you headed back to Georgia as soon as you came into your cupidity."

"No, that was not to be. The inheritance was, though. That and ma encounter with the rider of the pale horse."

So long ago. Hard to remember. Hard . . . to . . . remember.

1

Western & Atlantic Depot
Atlanta, Georgia
September 1873

Gathered on the platform, under a blazing sun in sweltering heat, Ah see remnants of a youthful life about to be taken from me by disease. Ah returned from St. Louis to claim Mother's share of Grandmother's estate. It would serve Ah thought to begin ma practice of dentistry. Soon after Christmas in '72, Ah began to lose weight. Ah thought little of it until a persistent cough followed. Ah consulted ma uncle John Stiles Holliday, a physician. His examination by stethoscope confirmed the worst of our fears. Ah suffered from the onset of pulmonary tuberculosis, the disease that claimed Mother's life some years before. Dr. John recommended drier climes of the west as being restorative to ma health. We placed our hopes in that, determined to fight the disease with all the vigor of youth. And so, Ah stand there on the platform, surrounded by family and pleasant memory about to depart to new life.

For the most part, ma early years were those of a happy childhood. A life of privilege, until Mother passed. We then endured the hardships of the war years. What is left to me of kin have come to see me off.

Father stands there, hat in hand as he should. Ah'm surprised he came. Perhaps a show of some remorse, though Ah doubt it. Henry Burroughs Holliday married a woman scarcely older than Ah. Married young Rachel under a scandalous cloud of suspicion before Mother's bones grew cold in the grave. Ah could not remain under the same roof with the odor of adultery fouling the air. Ah loved Mother far too much to tolerate such betrayal. Fortunately, education gave me reason to leave. Ah moved to Atlanta to live with ma aunt and uncle.

Ma uncle, Dr. John, previously introduced, encouraged ma interest in dentistry as a profession. A man of medicine, he reasoned dentistry to be clinically more advanced than his own profession for its enlightened use of anesthetics in surgical procedures. Medical boards of the time gave no credit to anesthesia in dealing with pain.

Ah owed him a debt from infancy for seeing to the surgical repair of ma cleft pallet defect done by the hands of the finest surgeon to be found for the procedure.

Uncle John is accompanied by his lovely wife, Aunt Permelia Ellen Ware Holliday. Ah dare say Ah loved her second only to Mother for the kindness and care with which she received me into her home. Treated me in so many ways as her own son. She among the few Ah knew to truly understand the depth of ma loss. Not only for Mother but for Father's betrayal.

Ma cousin Robert Alexander Holliday stands beside Aunt Permelia. A cousin by kin, in truth we were more like brothers. Inseparable. Tall, slim, blond hair, blue eyes, and handsome. In those days we often were mistaken for brothers. Cugh, cugh. That was then of course. Uncle John gave us an old 1851 Navy Colt revolver. He insisted we learn to shoot. Good he did, as we shall see, marksmanship has saved ma life more times than Ah care to count. When Robert chose dental school, we planned a joint practice. That was before the rider of the pale horse took up ma trail. Best laid plans. . . .

Ma gaze next rests on Sophie. Dearest Sophie Walton, negro slave who nannied the children. Worldly wise she imparted lessons of common sense only gathered by life experiences other than those of the privileged classes. She taught us to play the negro gambling card game, called skinning. Two valuable skills came of those lessons. The game resembled faro, a tiger Ah bucked as a professional gambler. The other lesson you ask. Ah learned to count cards, playing for matchsticks. Cheap lesson. Valuable ability at a poker table. More than valuable when the stakes are high.

Lastly Ah come to Mattie. Golden curls, eyes so soft Ah might have gladly drowned in them. Skin of porcelain, a voice to soothe a raging soul, and lips to stir a young man's heart to flame. Mattie dearest of all. We grew up kindred spirits. Close cousins. In time we grew to love deeply. Scarcely dared admit it to ourselves, lest anyone suspect, though we knew. Love and longing so strong it pained. Cousins were known to wed in the old south but not in the Holliday clan. Tragic love, forbidden by blood and strictures of her Catholic faith. Social mores denied requite to our love, but what remains in our hearts to this very day cannot be denied. Always it is there between us. Unspoken embers, between the lines of the letters we pen.

"All aboard for Chattanooga!"

Dallas called, leaving joy and sorrow, love, and life in the past. Ah did not know it at the time. Ah thought Ah would return. Robert and Ah had our plans. The horseman had another plan.

Entrained
September 1873
Ah shouldered ma loss and boarded the train with some sense of excitement. Ah had been introduced to Dr. John A. Seeger, late of Georgia by letter of recommendation from Uncle John. Dr. Seeger responded with an offer of a position in his newly established dental practice in Dallas. The prospect of hanging ma professional shingle at long last came with the promise of independence and a prosperous new life of ma own making. Firstly, the journey must be negotiated.

Rail service developed rapidly in the years following the war. The transcontinental route completed in 1869. From that major artery, regional lines spread like life giving veins feeding the nation settlement and prosperity. From Chattanooga, Ah entrained to Memphis and on to Jackson, Mississippi, and New Orleans. Here Ah paused to taste the creole comforts of the city, renowned for Andrew Jackson's defeat of the British in 1814. Had that southern general not fought so brilliantly and prevailed, the west Ah hoped to reach might well have fallen to the British, and the land we so richly cherish might well have taken on a dramatically different cultural aspect.

From New Orleans, Ah traveled by rail to Morgan City, Louisiana, and on to Beaumont, Texas, by stage. Here Ah shall pause ma tale. Travel by stagecoach is a filthy, dirty, painful ordeal. Ah had the advantage of a first-class seat, allowing me a place inside the coach, as opposed to third-class passengers who rode on the roof and second-class passengers who, while accorded a seat inside, might be asked along with the third class passengers to get out and push over difficult stretches of road. Then there is the matter of the seats themselves. Padded horsehair whose comfort is the horse's revenge on those who mistreated them in life. What's more, six passengers wedged onto benches comfortable to accommodate four. All that humanity packed into a hot, dusty confine defiled the air, aggravating ma condition. The only relief to be had taken from the comforts of whiskey. A comfort largely unknown to ma formative years. A comforting necessity to deflect advances of the horseman following behind.

In Beaumont, Ah partook a hotel bed, a bath, and a decent meal though not in that order. The following morning Ah entrained once more for Houston and on to Dallas, The whole of the journey spanning two weeks.

2

Dr. John A. Seeger, DDS
56 Elm Street
Dallas, Texas

Railroad development drove growth and prosperity in north Texas much as it did wherever the rails opened a town to wider vistas of commerce. Stepping off the train, Ah was swallowed up in blustery bustle not quite yet grown into itself. The first order of business, find ma new partner. Dr. Seeger maintained his practice in a two-room office above Cochrane's Drug Store. The smaller outer office served reception and patient waiting. Ah found the good doctor in the inner examination and treatment room, sterilizing instruments in preparation for the day's patients.

"Doctor Seeger, John Henry Holliday at your service."

"Welcome, Doctor Holliday. We've been expecting you. I hope you had a pleasant and uneventful journey."

"Eventfully long though not altogether unpleasant, and please call me John."

"And as a colleague, you must return the favor of calling me John."

"John we are then."

"I see you have your instrument case. You'll find a storage cupboard in the cabinet." He gestured to an upright bureau with lower drawers, work surface counter, and upper storage. "We've only one chair, unless you brought your own."

"Ah did not."

"Then we shall have to schedule patients accordingly. Well, that seems to cover things for the moment. Settle yourself in. I'm sure my wife, Martha, will want to properly welcome you to Dallas with dinner this evening."

As matters would unfold, it wasn't the best of times to open a new dental practice in Dallas or Texas for that matter. Rapid growth fueled by railroad expansion leveled off leading up to and following ma arrival. Prosperity and growth move in lockstep. Ah was new to the city and came to believe ma disease off putting to some prospective new patients. Faced with the necessity of bills to pay and meager funds remaining after travel and living expenses, Ah found Ah might buttress ma income at gaming tables in the Alhambra Saloon. There Ah was introduced to a game of chance similar to ma experience with the familiar game skinning. This time Ah did not play for matchsticks.

Alhambra Saloon
November 1873

The Alhambra introduced me to the western saloon. It was the beginning of a relationship Ah was to follow for the remainder of ma life. Saloons came in all sizes and styles, from tent-tops to elegant comique theaters. The Alhambra set a descent standard with a mirrored back bar and a spacious gaming concession lighted by chandeliers and wall sconces of simple design. Saloon atmosphere consisted of a haze of tobacco smoke, scent of stale beer, and a tin-pan piano playing in the background. Ambiance not well suited to ma condition became a necessity of supporting ma-self. Ma gaming education began at the tables.

The game of faro is known among the sporting class as bucking the tiger, for the image of a fearsome tiger pictured on the back of playing cards commonly used in the game. The game is played on a board, generally covered in green felt. A single suit of cards, most often spades, called the layout, are arranged on the board in numerical order from ace to king. A banker runs the game drawing cards from a box known as the shoe. The shoe contains a full deck of shuffled cards hidden from sight. The banker draws cards one at a time. Players, called punters, bet in multiple ways. The simplest bet places a player's chip, known as a check, on one of the thirteen cards in the layout. Checks varied in value from fifty cents to as much as ten dollars depending on the stakes of the banker's game. If the card drawn matched the punter's bet, the punter won. If another card was drawn, the house won the bet. Easy enough, Ah thought.

Multiple bets and betting strategies added spice to the game. A player might place multiple bets at varying values to temper risk. Bets could be placed on consecutive cards by placing a check between two cards. Bets could also be reversed by placing a copper token or penny on top of a bet. In this case the punter played with the banker, winning if the copper bet lost.

The banker began a new game by drawing one card called the soda first. This leaves fifty-one cards in the shoe for the play of the game. The banker next draws two cards, the first the banker's card, the second the player's card. A player who bet on the banker's card, lost. The player's card was the winning card. All bets on that card were paid dollar for dollar. The banker settled bets after each two cards drawn, allowing players to adjust their bets or add new ones. This continues until three cards remain in the shoe. The banker then announces, "the turn." This calls for a special bet on the sequence in which the three cards are drawn, the banker, the player, and the hock. In this bet, the player card paid five to one, the hock four to one, unless a pair were drawn. A pair paid one to one.

After observing the game for a time, Ah began to see opportunity form, though not from ma ability to count cards as Ah had expected. An abacus-like device called a casekeep served to keep players alert to the odds and eliminate the advantage of those who might count, including the banker. The casekeep featured a four-bead counter for each denomination in the layout. As cards were drawn, beads were passed leaving the remaining cards in the denomination visible to all. Ah saw betting strategy an advantage Ah might exploit, placing straight bets where odds appeared favorable and copper bets where odds appeared poor. Ah used the strategy as Ah began to play, though Ah must say success was modest in the beginning and came at the expense of more than a few lessons in the school of hard knocks.

Among those hard lessons Ah soon learned most games are rigged. Cheating is rampant in faro, rising to an art form in the fingers of some bankers. Bankers used trick shoes and marked cards to improve their control of the game. Dealing pairs, for example the house splits bets on those cards totaling the sum of the pair, thereby improving the banker's odds in the game. Allowing for the expectation of cheating, Ah was able to improve ma odds with betting strategies using coppers and card sequences known to remain in the shoe. Four beads remaining in the casekeep for consecutive denominations might invite an aggressive bet or a copper when odds on the sequence tilted less than even. Perhaps ma most important observation found the surest way to win at faro was to bank the game.

Gambling came with a companion vice. Whiskey. Ah found ma taste for it, after "medicinal" use on the stage ride. Moderate at first, but as is the case with such indulgences, fondness grows stronger. The more time Ah spent at the tables, the more time Ah spent with a whiskey glass by ma side. Ma tolerance for strong drink increased in the weeks and months in which 1873 turned to 1874. Ah found Ah could maintain a pleasant state of inebriation sufficient to ease the discomforts of disease without impairing ma ability to remain competitive at the gaming tables. That of course is a delicate balance to sustain over any extended period of time, but those discoveries lay in the future.

The only material set back Ah experienced as a consequence of gambling somewhat professionally, other than the losses one might expect, came to ma practice of dentistry. A paucity of patients occasioned by ma health, the irregularity of ma hours, and Dr. Seeger's disapproval of ma consumption of alcohol all led to dissolution of our partnership in March of the new year. The brevity of our professional association made for some awkward explanation where Uncle John and the family were concerned, though Ah assured them Ah saw greater opportunity in striking out on ma own.

Ah made a show of setting up a private dental practice but in all honesty only for a show of respectability. Ah felt the need of respectability for the sake of family appearances. To be sure, gambling is an honorable recreation for a refined southern gentleman but not something regarded as a decent profession. Ah felt Ah owed the Holliday name somewhat more. More to the point ma gaming skills and new found financial resources prepared me to step up ma game to Johnny Thompson's variety theater, home to Dallas's high stakes gamblers.

3

Johnny Thompson's Variety Theater
Dallas 1874

With dentistry reduced to the appearance of respectability, gambling became ma primary source of self-support. High stakes games offered greater reward, accompanied by risk of greater losses. A few months play at Variety Theater taught me the best chance of improving ma professional lot at high stakes tables could be found in banking ma own game. Ah continued to buck the tiger while contemplating the next step in ma new career and preparing ma-self to bank a game. While still a player, another new chapter opened to life as a professional gambler.

At the time, Ah was generally aware gambling ordinances existed. No one paid them much mind as they were seldom enforced. Ah soon learned these ordinances became enforceable when city treasuries found themselves in need of cash. As the economic boom brought on by railroad expansion contracted, city fathers turned to ordinance enforcement for tax relief. The turn in policy, led to ma first arrest.

Arrest itself was a trifle of an inconvenience. One appears before a magistrate, charged with betting on a faro bank, for which a fine of ten dollars is assessed. Had it ended there, Ah should have counted it no more than a cost of doing business. Unfortunately, such matters did not end at the courthouse. Local dailies routinely reported civil disobediences recorded on the police blotter. Ah found lurid articles blaring "prominent local dentist arrested for illegal gambling" deleterious to ma aura of respectability. Should word of such a misadventure reach Atlanta, the family would be horrified at such behavior sullying the Holliday name. Ah had no desire to bring disgrace upon those Ah loved. Ah determined to make right of it by correcting the record before it could so much as be encountered.

Ah wrote ma dearest Mattie, informing her of a dreadful mistake appearing in one or more of the Dallas dailies. It seems a gambler going by the name J. Holliday was arrested for violating the city's gaming

29

ordinance. The reporter having confused the itinerant gambler with J. H. Holliday, prominent dentist, reported the arrest in error. Ah assured her Ah demanded publication of a retraction but entrusted to her the truth she might use to clear confusion should word of the mistaken identity reach the family. Ah closed with deepest affection and the hope the whole regrettable misunderstanding would not trouble the family in any way.

Thoughts of ma beloved Mattie came with painful memories of home — scars of Father's betrayal and a life taken from me by the fickle finger of fateful disease all of which Ah sought to keep buried beneath a whiskey haze. Ma infirmity provided constant reminder of the disease that took Mother and snuffed out ma childhood before Ah was old enough to give it up willingly.

Then there was Father. The man lacked the decency to honor Mother's memory for so much as a year. His marriage made a mockery of mourning. For no fault of her own, Ah could not abide the woman. She deprived me of ma home for the satisfactions of Father, satisfactions likely preceding Mother's passing.

Lastly, Ah had to confront the sorry state

of ma dental career. Robert and Ah planned a partnership in Atlanta. This, too, the disease would take from me. These angers simmered beneath the surface of ma demeanor, fueling a hot temper Ah could not deny. Looking back Ah might have seen trouble brew in strong drink, distemper, and ma next accommodation to life in the west.

Westerners went about armed as naturally as the clothing they wore. Particularly so in saloons and gambling parlors. Ah determined it prudent to carry a suitable firearm. Ah settled on an 1872 .41 Colt pocket pistol for its compact size, ease of concealment and carry, along with passable accuracy at close range for a short, barreled weapon. Over the years ma preference in pistols would evolve in style and efficiency, though the '72 served ma purpose in 1874.

Outfitting ma-self with a bank began with the San Francisco firm of Will & Fink's catalog. Ah selected a layout of modest design, not wanting to give the appearance of a "slick" game. The shoe too, Ah kept simple, no mechanics to be caught on close inspection. Cards, a delicate touch, and the aid of a little "skinning," reminiscent of Sophie, provided all the edge needed to improve ma odds and take on the game.

Once the layout arrived, Ah spent nearly

as much time practicing the deal as Ah did bucking the tiger. Ah meant to be so proficient a banker as to make ma players comfortable with the odds allowed. If betting strategies could be used to improve a punter's odds, cheating strategies improved the appearance of a game's "integrity." Modestly calculated returns on the stakes could be had, short of a greedy take for the house. Lady Luck should have seating on both sides of the table, though one somewhat more comfortable than the other.

As 1874 came to a close, Ah took stock of the changes ma time in Dallas had wrought. Dentistry no longer provided the sustenance of life. Ah admitted to being well on the way to, if not already accomplished, the life of a professional gambler. Ah had the wherewithal to bank ma own game. Then too, Ah still suffered demons past, prodding any measure of contentment. Ah felt restless. Wanderlust some might call it. Ah moved north to Denison for a time. The town, too small, failed to satisfy. Ah craved more action. Another affliction to haunt ma disease ridden soul. Colorado beckoned.

Spring 1875
Ah left Dallas when the weather warmed to avoid the discomforts of winter travel and

the worst of summer heat whilst traveling by stage. Ma route of travel proceeded west to Fort Worth and Fort Griffin where Ah stopped briefly to gamble and drink at Owen Donnelly's Beehive saloon. Owen was a man Ah befriended from ma earliest days at the Alhambra. Fort Griffin enjoyed a prominent point of demarcation on the new western cattle trail with the prosperity brought by vast cattle herds headed up the trail to railhead in Kansas and the thirsty cowboys who drove them there. Fort Griffin would be the drovers last watering hole for weeks on the trail.

With a few dollars added to ma pockets, Ah continued west to El Paso and north to Las Vegas, New Mexico, where Ah again paused to refresh ma-self from the rigors of travel. From Las Vegas the Santa Fe trail wound its way northeast into Colorado by way of Wooten's Toll Road over Raton Pass. Richens Lacy Wooten, better known as Uncle Dick, built the road along with a hotel and restaurant that served as a pleasant stage stop at the southern base of the pass.

The Colorado stage route crossed the pass with stops in Trinidad, and Pueblo. As Ah have previously recounted, Ah held stage travel in low opinion for all its discomforts.

That said, Ah was enthralled by the grandeur and vistas passing by the coach windows as we climbed and switched our way over the mountains. Sunrises, bright and blue, evenings, orange and crimson, purple in shadow. Breathtaking for what little breath there was to be had at those altitudes for one such as Ah.

The mountains evoked feelings of spirituality long lost since the days Mother taught me her faith. Ah admit to having neglected godly ways since briefly joining a Methodist church upon ma arrival in Dallas. The Creator felt present to me in the mountains. A presence Ah would have been well advised to hold on to. Perhaps Ah should have, had it not been for the pale horseman following so close.

Theatre Comique
Denver

Ah found favorable concession for ma game at Theatre Comique, adopting the alias Tom Mackey as a precaution against any lingering Texas reputation tainting ma new circumstances. A genteel establishment, the Theatre featured vaudeville acts, a saloon, and gambling parlor. Ah stuck to ma game with a light thumb on the scales for the bank. In so doing, Ah avoided any trouble or activity as might confront the law while attracting a following of some of Denver's more prominent sports.

In '75, table talk swirled around a gold strike discovered by Colonel George A. Custer on an exploratory expedition in the Black Hills near Deadwood in South Dakota. A Yankee of dubious repute, Custer surely created his share of a stir by his discovery. A gold rush ensued, igniting Lakota war drums. The Sioux held the Black Hills, sacred center of their nation and land ceded to them by the Fort Laramie Treaty of 1868. White men were not welcome. Gold would abrogate any treaty promised the Indian.

Cheyenne
July 1876
Denver and Ah could not long resist a seduction siren song as strong as gold. Cheyenne made home to Union Pacific transcontinental rail service, supplying store for gold seekers on their way to the gold fields. It made for a gambler's paradise. In picking up stakes and moving ma game to Cheyenne, Ah did little more than follow prosperous punters who left Denver for the golden pleasures of Cheyenne. Ah arrived in Cheyenne February 1876, and attached

ma game to Tom Miller's Bella Union gaming concession.

In June the army was called in to bring the warring tribes to heel. In a twist of irony, Colonel Custer, the Yankee who arguably started the war, paid for it with his life and the lives of the men under his command. The Sioux victory at the Little Big Horn served only to stiffen national will to see the tribes held to account.

Soon after the Custer tragedy, table talk returned to the gold boom in Deadwood. A siren song, sung each evening at the tables in Cheyenne. By Fall of that year, Tom moved Bella Union to Deadwood to be closer to action in gold dust and nuggets.

4

Deadwood
September 1876

Deadwood came by its name honestly. The sliver of a tent-top town with a handful of clapboard buildings clung to the muddy walls of a steep gulch overlooked by a stand of dead pine trees, raised like bars to a prison fence. Thus, the name. All else honest could be checked at the outskirts of town.

Deadwood's version of the Bella Union proved far less "Bella" for, shall we say, more primitive conditions than those we enjoyed in Cheyenne. Still the money was there and freely flowing, as generous as the creeks carrying dust and nuggets to busy pans.

Early one evening, as Ah sat at ma layout waiting for players to arrive, Ah became aware of a presence looming over me. Ah glanced upon a fine figure of a man, well made and handsome with clear eyes and a full mustache.

"Care to play," Ah asked.

"I may. You run a square game?"

"Square as the law allows. John Henry Holliday at your service."

"Wyatt. Wyatt Earp."

"Pleased to meet you, Wyatt Earp. Have a seat."

He took the offered seat. "Care for a drink? On the bank."

"Thanks, no. Don't drink much. Never when I play."

"Mind if I do? At least until we have enough to bank a game."

"Suit yourself."

Ah lifted ma glass in toast. "Man of few words."

"Been told."

"Where you from, Wyatt?"

"Does it matter?"

"Not really. Just exchanging get acquainted pleasantries."

"How long you been away from Georgia?"

Ah smiled. "The dulcet tones of ma cultured speech hath given me away once more."

"Hath? My ear give you away."

"What brings you to Deadwood, sir, apart from the pleasure of ma company, that is?"

"Same as brings you. Gold."

"You don't strike me as the mining type."

"Makes us even."

"How so?"

"You strike me as a gambler."

"Given away yet again. Course you do have the advantage of me by ma sitting here banking a faro layout."

With that, players began to arrive, and Ah opened a game. Wyatt Earp played that evening and became something of a regular. A taciturn man of sober demeanor, we developed an easy friendship over the winter in spite of our differences. A friendship destined to have a profound effect on what remained of ma life in coming years, though at the time we had no way to know what lay beyond the grey mists of future.

Hotel Glenwood
Glenwood Springs, Colorado
September 1887

Kate handed me fresh linen to replace the blood-stained kerchief Ah'd put to overuse. She returned to the chair beside ma bed at the window, cast in a glow of golden light. She might have been seen for an angel in times like these.

"Profound effect indeed," she said. "The profound effect of that friendship overflowed with profound effects for both of us. I can't help wondering what we might have become were it not for that friendship."

"We had our love story to this very day." Ah passed her ma glass for a refill.

"Love and war be closer to the truth." She poured.

"Spice of life, darlin'. All's well that ends well."

"This is all ending well?"

"For so long as we have this time together." Ah took a swallow.

"This here is the ending come in no small measure from the time you befriended that man. Deadwood no less. Some poetry to that if a person were fond of poetic tragedy."

"Tragedy? Ah shouldn't think so. Looks like high adventure from where Ah sit."

Breckenridge, Texas
July 4, 1877
In the spring of '77, Ah returned to Texas by way of Cheyenne, Denver, and Kansas City. Ah made brief stays in Dallas and Dennison before following the sports on to the town of Breckenridge west of Fort Worth. Breckenridge attracted sporting crowd action by a law enforcement atmosphere somewhat more relaxed than those having taken possession of towns like Dallas

40

and Fort Worth. Respectability laden reformers placed a heavy burden on the gambling profession. Less rigid enforcement of gaming ordinances did nothing to reduce the physical risks of professional gambling. The pale horseman passed close by that Independence Day, though not from his stranglehold grip on ma lungs.

Early that afternoon Ah chanced to sit in on a poker game among whose players seated local card sharp Henry Kahn. The game proceeded satisfactorily enough though not heavily in ma favor for some time. Kahn's fortunes being not well served in the early going, he endeavored to change his luck by his next turn at the deal. He shuffled the deck and cut it in a manner giving rise to mistrust.

"Suh, if you would, let's see that deck cut again."

He responded with a glare. "You sayin' I cheated, Holliday?"

"No, suh, Ah merely prefer a less deliberate cut of the cards."

"What's cut is cut."

He began to deal. Ah rapped the table smartly with ma walking stick. "Ah believe Ah requested you re-cut the cards."

"And I said what's cut is cut. You plan to make something of it," he said rising from his chair.

Somewhat bigger than Ah, Ah saw no advantage to a barroom brawl. When he came around the table toward me Ah took ma walking stick to him, administering a proper thrashing if Ah do say so ma-self. Ah had not quite beaten the starch out of him when the police arrived. We were both arrested and fined. Ah thought that put an end to the matter.

Early that evening as Ah left the diner where Ah had taken ma supper, Kahn accosted me on the board walk. Ah advised him if he were not careful, Ah would finish the caning he so richly deserved. Where upon in a most ungentlemanly display he drew his pistol and fired. Ah was struck down, grievously wounded, though for a mercy not mortally so. A nearby policeman quickly disarmed Kahn and arrested him before he could finish his murderous intent.

A doctor was summoned. He was able to staunch the bleeding and see me conveyed to a space in his office reserved for hospital care. Thanks to prompt and competent medical attention, Ah embarked down a long painful road to recovery. Surgically repaired bullet wounds to the chest do not comport well with a tubercular cough such as mine. Even with the aid of laudanum, the pain brought on by ma cough gave exclamation to the direction of ma disease. Time passed slowly as Ah regained strength on a rough road to recovery.

Word of ma situation reached the family in Atlanta. Ma cousin, George Henry Holliday, came out from Atlanta at family behest to see to my wellbeing. By the time he arrived, Ah had moved to the Transcontinental Hotel in Fort Worth. We had a most pleasant visit, during which George Henry brought news of the family and all the comforts of home. He did his best to encourage me to return to Atlanta with him, expressing Robert's invitation to join him in his thriving dental practice. As much as that dream tugged at ma heartstrings, Ah knew dentistry to be beyond a man in ma condition. Then of course there was the news of ma forbidden love Mattie. Having heard God's call, my love entered a Sisters of Charity convent, becoming the nun now known as Sister Mary Melanie. Ah suppressed ma surprise and the true nature of ma feelings. For once the cough served useful purpose. It gave cover and convincing weight to the futility of any thought of returning to Georgia. Ah expressed ma regrets to Robert at not being able to return with him. Ah bid him thank you, thank you and goodbye aware of the finality in that farewell. Ah was never to return. Nothing remained for me there.

Here Ah pause ma tale for Kate's benefit in thought. Robert brought with him a letter from Mattie, explaining her decision to enter the order. Ah cherished the scent of her words. Ah could conjure up the sound of her voice in reading and rereading it along with a vision of the curve to her slender neck. Homesick, lovesick, Ah treasured it. Ah have it. Locked away in the memory of the heart.

We turned the calendar over to August at George Henry's departure. He returned to Atlanta with word of ma recovery while Ah turned West to Fort Griffin and an unexpected reunion.

5

Fort Griffin, Texas
August 1877

Ah arrived in Griffin in late summer. Much had changed since ma last visit. Lawless elements had taken the community to the brink of chaos, resulting in the rise of law and order by vigilance committee whose brand of enforcement might best be described as lawless. Lynching became the common and swift response to rampant rustling. Ah took residence at Planters Hotel a block east of Shanny Shannesey's Cattle Exchange Saloon where Ah could bank ma faro game or play at poker should Ah wish.

Ah first met the lovely and charming Mary Katherine Horony in St. Louis during ma brief dentistry apprenticeship there in 1872. *Ah include reference to her beauty and charms as Ah know her to be listening.* She admitted being new to her profession, though Ah judged her suitably accomplished for a young man of ma limited experience in the intimacies of the fairer sex. Ah digress. She went by the name of Kate Fisher in those days. She had a delicate girlish side to her then, the rigors of the sporting life having yet to harden her. We took more than carnal pleasure from the time we spent together. She seemed fascinated by the prospects afforded me by ma dental profession. Our time in St. Louis was brief as Ah was to return home that summer to claim inheritance to ma mother's estate and bitter news of ma diagnosis.

We reacquainted in Griffin when she approached ma game early one evening in Shannesey's.

"Well, I declare, if it isn't the distinguished dentist Doctor John Henry Holliday."

Ah took her in. A few years older than Ah recalled. Profession toughened some by now. Still that mischievous, girlish glint in her eye. "Why, Miss Kate Fisher, if ma eyes don't deceive."

"Fisher then, Elder now, no matter. Your eyes do not deceive. What is this, dealin' faro? I thought you'd have yourself a respectable dental practice by now."

Cugh, cugh. Ah brought ma ever-present handkerchief to ma lips. "Dentistry is not to be for one in ma condition."

"I see. I'm sorry to hear that, John Henry. I had such high hopes for you back in St. Louis. Hopes you had too."

She said it truly sorry. "It's life, Kate. And then you die."

"It is, isn't it."

Like a rose by any other name, Kate was still Kate and all as Ah remembered her. Oh, she could be coarse when the need arose, yet she remained bright, with an appreciation for the finer indulgences of life, unusual for women in her profession. We bantered. We conversed. Ah enjoyed her company as she it seemed enjoyed mine. She became ma companion and luck charm at the faro bank Ah opened each night at Shanny's place. Ah do not now recall if she dubbed me the sobriquet, "Doc." If not, she saw it to permanence in life beyond dental practice.

Another faro game popular with Fort Griffin's sports was banked by the lovely Lottie Deno. She dealt an accomplished game packaged with auburn curls, slow green eyes, ruby lips, a throaty laugh, and alabaster skin filled out in all the most fetching places. Little wonder she won. Her sports had to keep in mind of the game. She fancied herself the best player around. Ah took it for ma duty to disabuse her of such a notion, there being room for only one best player around. She must have seen it her way the night she approached ma game. She wore a revealing green satin gown, tantalizingly trimmed in cinnamon lace at the bodice, Ah noticed. Kate noticed too. Ah felt a chill at ma back.

"They say you're pretty good, Holliday."

"Some say the same of you, Miss Deno."

"Mind if I sit in for some?"

"Ma pleasure, Miss Deno."

"Lottie will do."

"Then Ah must be Doc to you."

"Deal, Doc."

Ah did and with no thumb on the scale. One cannot cheat a professional dealer. They have seen all the tricks and practiced them too. Lottie Deno lived up to her reputation. She made a healthy dent in ma bank that night. Closing out a game late in the evening, she fixed me with a long lashed smoky gaze.

"I believe I've taken enough from you for the night, Doc. Come by anytime and have a hand at my game."

The invitation suggested there might be more to her game than faro. She got up to leave, stopping by the bar for a drink. Kate sidled up to her elbow. Ah could not hear what was said. At least not at first. The argument erupted in shrieks of most unladylike slurs. Ah thought it amusing Ah might be the source of their disagreement until Kate reached in her handbag and drew out a derringer. Ah stepped between them without hesitation, relieving Kate of her gun.

"Welcome to him," Lottie said on her way out the door.

"And you'll not be trying your hand at her game, Doc Holliday."

"Why Kate, darlin', Ah do believe you may be jealous." Toughened up some. Did Ah mention she could be coarse?

Hotel Glenwood
Glenwood Springs, Colorado
September 1887

"Ah, Griffin, Texas, I remember well," Kate gazed off at some distant vision. "And that slut, what was her name?"

"Lottie Deno?"

"That's the one. You *would* remember, wouldn't you?"

"Pretty fair faro player as Ah recall."

"And that's not *all* you recall, as I recall."

"Would you have shot her?"

"We'll never know, will we?"

"Saved you from yourself, Ah did."

"I might say the same."

"Ah should never have thought you the

49

jealous type, darlin' Kate."

"Nor should I. Just another of those great contradictions of nature come of my feelin's for you, John Henry. Confounding, you know. Scarcely understood myself at times."

"Owing to ma fascinating charm?"

"Fascinating charm? I make it more infuriating frustration."

"Love by another name."

She arched a brow. "Therein lies the frustration."

Cattle Exchange Saloon
October 1877

Ah sat at ma table early one evening waiting for players to arrive. A tall well-made man in a dark suit approached. Ah recalled Deadwood.

"Wyatt Earp, isn't it?"

"Good memory."

"What brings you to Fort Griffin?"

"Might ask you the same."

"Ma game. Your turn."

"Shanny said you might be able to help me."

"Help with what?"

"If you play with Texas cowboys who've been up Dodge City way, likely you heard of me from some of them."

"Texas cowboys are most all Ah usually

play with. Now that Ah think about it, though, Ah do remember some talk about a lawman by the name of Earp. Never connected it with you until now. You the law in Dodge City?"

He nodded.

"Now what would Dodge City law want with the likes of me? Ah've never been to Dodge."

"Not workin' Dodge City law just now. I'm a railroad detective for Union Pacific. Lookin' for some Texas boys padded their pockets up in Nebraska robbin' one of their trains."

"Padded their pockets?"

"Sixty thousand in gold. Guess you could call that padding."

"Guess you could. Not that Ah mind, but what of that brings you to ma game?"

"Shanny thought you might have picked up table talk from some of your players."

"In ma experience, those who rob trains are seldom given to confession if you know what Ah mean."

"The leader of the outfit is a man by the name of Sam Bass. Ever heard of him?"

"Can't say as Ah have. If you stay and play, we may be able to tease something out of one of these north Texas boys. Care for a drink?"

"Don't drink as a rule."

"That's right. Ah forgot." Ah poured. "Ah still do." Cugh, cugh.

"I see that. That why you gamble?"

"The disease? Bad for business in dentistry, I'm afriad. How do you know Shanny?"

"Laid track together one season. Made side money bettin' on him in bareknuckle boxing matches. He taught me some pugilistic arts. Right useful in law doggin'."

"That explains it."

"Explains what?"

"How he keeps such a tight lid on this place." With that Kate arrived.

"Evening, Doc."

"And you, Kate darlin'. Meet ma friend, Wyatt Earp."

"I know Wyatt Earp. Worked for Bessie Earp, James Earp's wife in Wichita. Worked for Tom Sherman in Dodge City before Tom found our way to Sweetwater and Fort Griffin. I know the Earps all right."

Wyatt looked her up and down. "Can't say I remember."

"Course you can't. All them high and mighty airs bein' too good for the likes of me."

Ah sensed some tension here best left to itself. Ah should have paid closer attention as time would reveal.

Wyatt stayed and played that night. By discrete inquiries we were unable to further his pursuit of the train robber. While he remained in town he'd come by for supper or an early evening visit. We renewed what must have seemed an unlikely friendship. Wyatt came from a large, closely knit family. In that we found common fabric. Kate expressed her disapproval by staying away when Wyatt was around. Ah enjoyed his company and saw no need to indulge her dislike. When she voiced her objection to the time Ah spent with Wyatt, Ah admit to having lost ma temper a time or two. Perhaps more. We could both be high strung. Did Ah mention coarse?

Hotel Glenwood
Glenwood Springs, Colorado
September 1887

"High strung and coarse is it," she mused.

"One way to put it."

"Are you going to persist in reliving the whole of this sordid story?"

"Passes the time. Isn't all so sordid as you say. Except those parts where you and Wyatt are concerned."

"If you are going to march us down miles of memory lane, I shall have more than enough opportunity to vent my views on his majesty, Wyatt Earp."

"Ah believe Ah have heard most of them."

"Likely you have, but if we are to continue reminiscing like this, you shall have the pleasure of hearing all of them again and then some. The best thing to be said about his visit to Griffin, it didn't last long enough to cause any real trouble."

6

Cattle Exchange
Saloon

On the eve of his departing Fort Griffin for his return to Dodge City, Wyatt paid me a visit to wish me farewell. With players yet to arrive Ah was pleased to have his company. We took seats in the tawny glow of early evening sun filtered through grime encrusted window glass. Ah gave ma whiskey a mellow amber swirl.

"What brings you by?"

"Pullin' out early in the mornin'."

"Back to Dodge?"

"Back to Dodge. You know you could find a right fine home for your game in Dodge. Cattle season brings in drovers flush with three month's pay. A good bit of it gets left at the tables, leastwise the part don't go to the doves and whiskey."

"Ah shall consider it."

"Do. I'd enjoy having you around, and

with all the pretty whores in town, a gentleman such as yourself could do right well on that score, too."

He said it with veiled reference to Kate. Plainly the two did not mix. Ah rose to shake his hand and watched him depart, thinking Ah shall miss his company.

Wyatt's invitation proved timely, though Ah did not know it at the time. It gave me some insight into Kate's antipathy toward Wyatt and her unpleasant recollections of Dodge. Ah doubted either would be easily overcome. In that conclusion Ah was destined to be proven right.

Cattle Exchange Saloon
January 1878

Ah engaged that night dealing a gentlemanly game of poker. Among the players the man on my right Ed Bailey sought to improve his luck by reminding himself of the content of the discard pile. Ah reminded him such a practice is a breach of etiquette by first offense, rising to cheating by the second. Further to the practice, it neutralizes advantage to those of us who remember the cards played and able to count the odds remaining in the game. As dealer Ah could not abide allowing the man the practice. At his third attempt, Ah claimed the pot for ma own without showing ma hand. A claim well within the rights of one aggrieved by flagrant cheating.

Bailey went for his gun in violation of a city ordinance against carrying a firearm. Ma boot knife slashed his chest, disarming the threat.

Shanny sent for the town marshal. He placed me under "house arrest" in the confines of my hotel room, allowing as how a magistrate was needed to establish authenticity of ma claim of self-defense. That may have settled the matter, save for the menace raised by Bailey's many friends.

Kate got wind of their plan to visit vigilante justice on ma person. She assessed the situation dire. With the mob fortifying itself with liquid courage and a young city deputy on guard outside ma room at the Planter's Hotel, she determined our situation in need of a diversion.

Clever girl secured two horses on which to make our escape. She then set fire to a shed behind the saloon, sounding the fire alarm. With the mob pressed to serve as fire brigade to douse the flames. Kate next entered the hotel, diverting the city guard first by her feminine charms and then by means of his colt revolver.

Having secured my release, we bound and

gagged the young officer and fled into the night to the waiting horses. We mounted up and rode out of town, long gone before the fire could be put out.

"Now what," Kate said in a breath of steam as we rode. "We surely cannot stay here."

"True." Ah pondered the question. Wyatt's invitation came to mind, though Ah knew better than to suggest such a thing to Kate in the midst of our current predicament. Ah determined discretion demanded the right moment.

"We shall have time enough to ponder a destination once we leave Fort Griffin behind.

Laredo, Texas

Dusty and windswept Laredo offered little by way of charm. It did offer respite. We stopped to rest the horses, take a few days at our trades to fatten our purses, and purchase supplies for the next leg of our journey. Ah judged Laredo far enough from Fort Griffin to reveal ma plan in the privacy of our hotel room.

"Dodge City! Why in hell would you want to go to that shithole?"

"Wyatt suggested ma game might do quite well there during the cattle season."

"Earp. I might have known. Why would you listen to that skull bustin' asshole?"

"That 'skull bustin' asshole,' as you so colorfully put it, is ma friend."

"Bad choice of friends."

"Ah shall be the judge of that. Why are you so peevish toward Wyatt? He spoke kindly of you."

"I seriously doubt that."

"Is it Wyatt you object to or some misadventure in Dodge City you chose to run away from?"

"He told you that!"

"Now, now, Mary Katherine, let's not get your corset in a knot."

"Don't you Mary Katherine *me*, Doc Holliday, lessen you want your skull busted."

"Threats of violence do not become a lady, Kate."

"I ain't no lady."

"At times such as this Ah believe we can agree on that. As for where we go from here, Ah am going to Dodge City, whether you care to come or not."

"You'd leave me here after I saved your sorry ass from a lynchin' bee?"

"For which Ah am most appreciative, however the choice before you is Dodge

City or wherever Texas tumble weeds take you."

"You ungrateful son-of-a-bitch, I don't know why I put up with you."

"You love me for ma intellect and charm."
Cugh, cugh.

"Cough up a lung full of charm. The west is full of places your game will play. How about Colorado?"

"What will it be? Dodge City or" — Ah glanced around — "Laredo."

"Son-of-a-bitch."

"Excellent choice."

Hotel Glenwood
Glenwood Springs, Colorado
September 1887
Ah rested while Kate went out for some supper. She returned as shadows stretched into evening. She brought with her a bowl of soup and a generous slice of fresh bread. She propped me up and lit the bedside lamp for us.

"Now eat. You need your strength."

Ah dipped a bit of bread in the soup. It warmed me, though Ah had little appetite.

"Clever girl. I was, wasn't I?"

"Ah seem to recall acknowledging that."

"Yes, you did, at least as to the fire that saved your life. Unlike advice where others are concerned."

By "others" she no doubt referred to Wyatt and his brothers. "Ah have never doubted your considerable intellect in which we both indulge in fascination." She favored me with a look of hers as good as pointing to where the bull shit. Ah smiled.

"You're right. It is past time to go there again."

"And there it is, intellect and indulgence."

"Now indulge me with some of that soup before it gets cold. And more than a bite of bread. I'll not have you starve to death on my watch."

"Watches over me like a hovering angel."

"No angel, either, Doc. Just the Kate in your life."

That said it in summation. The Kate in ma life. There could only be one Kate. The road ahead beckoned. We traveled much of it together.

Eagle Pass

Winter travel can be slow. We did it in legs, pausing along the way to stay a few days here and there, taking breaks from the weather or to fatten our purses from a few days' play. Kate took to this agreeably as she was in no hurry to return to Dodge and held out hope Ah might find a situation sufficiently agreeable to change ma plans. We nearly did in Eagle Pass.

Eagle Pass was a wide-open border town, affording business opportunities for both Kate and me. For her part, she could entertain as many customers as she wished on any given evening. Ah found dental work across the border at a Mexican army fort during the day and play at ma faro bank by night.

We continued our nomadic journey in this fashion, eventually reaching Dodge City just in time for beginning the cattle season.

7

Dodge City, Kansas
May 1878

Dodge appeared in the distance as we rode in from the south. Dunn dust smudged the horizon from the grazing grounds south and west of town and the cattle pens serving the Atchison Topeka & Santa Fe rail yard. Riding north on Bridge Street, cow-scented air hung in a dense haze impervious to the constancy of Kansas wind. Ah should have seen it for what it was. Air laden with dust and dried dung could not benefit ma condition. Ah should have seen it. Ah did not.

Front Street divided Dodge east to west along the tracks, respectable north of the tracks, rowdy south of a line known as the deadline. We would find opportunity on both sides of that line, but first, dog tired after weeks on the trail, accommodation became the necessity. Kate led the way east on Front Street, two blocks to Dodge

House. There we stabled our horses and took a room, too weary to take note of the amenities Dodge House afforded.

The following mid-day, after a good night's sleep, Ah discovered the dining room, bar, billiard parlor, and much to ma pleasant surprise, a laundry. Life on the western frontier imposed primitive hardships Ah endeavored to resist whilst maintaining a gentlemanly posture about ma attire. A coat of brushed gray flannel, fresh linen of subdued hue, and cravat accented by a stylish diamond stickpin being the apparel of the day and evening. Accommodations at Dodge House afforded me opportunity to hang out ma dentistry shingle, a service Ah soon learned lacking in the community. Ah had a respectable profession by day with vibrant gaming action by night. Dodge promised all the possibilities Wyatt suggested in spite of Kate's reservations.

Arrival of the AT&SF heralded Dodge City a boom town. Business along Front Street north of the tracks included grocery and general mercantile stores, a dance hall, café, blacksmith shop, tobacco shop, and saloons, Chalk Beeson's Long Branch being the most notable along with the Alhambra. What self-respecting boom town didn't need saloons? Self-respect had nothing to do with any town laying claim to boom reputation. The least pretense of self-respect checked itself south of the tracks with The Lady Gay and Lone Star saloons catering to the more raucous cowboy crowd. Ah played ma game in the latter establishments on the arrival of a new herd. The action at the tables at those times robust along with the risks of trail hardened cowboys blowing off steam. Apart from the arrival of new blood, blood spilled more than occasionally. Ah preferred playing ma game with the more refined players frequenting the Alhambra and Long Branch north of the deadline. They, too, played with the wealth of Texas money, though once removed from the rather rowdy original transfer.

We settled into Dodge society with introductions provided by Wyatt and the woman in his life, Mattie Blaylock. Common threads to this social circle were bound by law enforcement and gambling, Wyatt having taken a position as a city policeman, while adding to his meager wages at the gaming tables. Our social circle included Long Branch Saloon owners Bill Harris and Chalk Beeson, along with Luke Short who ran the Long Branch gaming concession. Wyatt befriended Ford County Sheriff W.B.

"Bat" Masterson and his brother Jim who served on the Dodge City police force with Wyatt. Given our evening occupations, Kate and Ah found advantage to both associations. Ah in gaming, Kate in law with Dodge having a lightly enforced ordinance prohibiting the oldest profession. Apart from professional considerations we found fellowship if not universal friendship as Kate maintained her cool demeanor toward Wyatt, though both endeavored to maintain an uneasy peace.

July 26, 1878
That season comedian Eddie Foy performed at the Lady Gay saloon and Comique Theater. One evening Ah took ma game south of the tracks to enjoy the diversion of his performance. Ah sat at ma game that night with Bat Masterson, who like Wyatt padded his income at the tables. We were well acquainted, though through a reserved relationship, Bat having a sober demeanor akin to Wyatt yet without the warmth. He was a competent lawman, handsome and well made. He possessed a fine intellect and a sharp command of the English language Ah respected as a badge of culture uncommon to the west. That evening we played well into the night.

In the early morning hours, shots rang out ripping gaping holes in the clapboard wall beside the stage. Foy dove out of the footlights as fast as Bat and Ah hit the floor.

Outside, the shots were fired by a cowboy riding south on Bridge Street. Wyatt, who was making his rounds as a city policeman, came running. The shooter galloped away. Wyatt fired twice, knocking the rider off his horse with the second shot. The cowboy, George Hoy, would die of his wound but not before confessing he'd meant to kill Wyatt for the one-thousand-dollar bounty offered for his death. Law and order earned more than casual disrespect among those in the cow camps and the wealthy Texas ranchers who employed them.

Lady Gay Saloon
August 18, 1878
Later that season another venture south of the tracks, chanced misadventure. Arrival of a herd up from the Texas King Ranch prompted ma game this night. Kate, too, took her enterprise to the Lady Gay. The King Ranch crew descended on the Lady Gay and proceeded to take over the bar. One of the cowboys, a surly young man with the rowdy demeanor of a ringleader, jumped behind the bar shoving the bartender out of

the way.

"Come-on boys! Drinks are on the house."

The crowd bellied up to the bar as the cowboy bartender passed out whiskey by the bottle.

"I'll have a beer," someone in the crowd shouted.

"Pour it yourself," the cowboy bartender laughed, tossing a glass to the man in the crowd.

The bartender, a solidly built fellow himself, elbowed his way through the crowd. "You," he shouted leveling a thick finger at the boy behind the bar. "Get the hell out of there before I call the marshal."

"Shut up, fat man. Don't you know who I am?"

"Don't know. Don't give a damn, either. Get your ass out of my bar."

"James Kenedy of the King Ranch Kenedys, that's who I am. Now shut your fat face before I buy this two-bit dump for the pleasure of burning it down."

"You tell 'em, Spike," someone called from the crowd.

Wyatt swung through the batwings taking stock of the situation. He buffaloed the first man he found at the end of the bar. Buffaloing was a practice used by the Earps and Masterson to subdue troublemakers, stopping short of gun violence. Well, not completely short. The practice rendered the miscreant unconscious by a blow to the head with the butt of a pistol. Thus disabled, the subject could be arrested and jailed for the evening with the privilege of living to recount the tale. Kenedy took offense at Wyatt presuming to arrest one of his fellows.

"What the hell do you think you're doing?"

"The arrest charge is disorderly conduct. Care to join him?"

"We'll see about that." Kenedy and several others followed Wyatt and his prisoner out to the street, surrounding him in threatening fashion.

Ah observed all this from ma seat at the table at which Ah played. Badly outnumbered and with no backup in sight, Ah feared Wyatt in peril. Ah asked to borrow the pistol of one of ma playing partners, which was graciously provided. Drawing ma own Colt Lightening, Ah stepped out to the boardwalk at the back of Kenedy and his men.

"Up with your hands!"

They turned as one to the deadly halos of two cocked six guns. Wyatt drew his gun. "You're all under arrest. Drop those gun belts nice and easy."

"Right this way, gentlemen." With Kenedy and his cowboys disarmed, Wyatt led. We marched them off to jail. After locking them up, Wyatt and Ah returned to the Lady Gay, where Ah returned the borrowed pistol.

"Come along, Doc. Let me buy you a drink."

"Not necessary. Ah merely meant to even the odds."

"Even the odds, hell. You likely saved my life."

Wyatt bought me a drink. He declined to join me for being on duty. More than a drink passed between us that night. Ah learned if a man had Wyatt Earp's back, that man has a friend for life. Ah was struck by that. It bespoke loyalty a man could count on no matter the circumstances. While Wyatt was no southerner, he evinced values of family, courage, and loyalty to do any southern gentleman proud. In the years that lay before us, the bond formed that evening on the wrong side of the deadline would be tested time and again, never to fail.

Hotel Glenwood
Glenwood Springs, Colorado
September 1887
Kate sat in ma bedside chair hands folded,

haloed in lamplight steeped in thought.

"You know, Doc, I well remember that night at the Lady Gay. I can't help but wonder what might have happened to us had you not taken it upon yourself to back up that man."

Ah thought some. "Wyatt may have been killed. He thought as much."

"He might have. Something changed that night. Something more than you saving his life."

"Very perceptive of you to note that." *Cugh, cugh . . . cugh.* "It made for a bond between us."

"Made one and broke the possibility of another. Now get some sleep."

She rose, huffed out the lamp, and retired to her room.

8

Kate recalling the Kenedy incident as she had left me lying awake starring into the darkness. For the profound change the events of that evening made on ma friendship with Wyatt, somewhat more should be said where Kate is concerned. We have long had a complex relationship, Kate and Ah. She, for her part, loved me. Ah had nothing to offer her beyond the prospect of ma ever imminent demise. That and a heart long given for another. Mattie. Love never to be. Kate had her profession. Ah accepted it as she accepted mine. Ma friendship with Wyatt and his brothers became a problem for her. She did not like Wyatt, nor did she approve of ma association with him. It bordered on jealousy over another woman which some might find amusing, given her occupation. Wyatt held Kate in low regard. He thought her overbearing and too intrusive in ma comings, goings, and doings. He it was who insinuated she had her "Big Nose" in ma business. The Big Nose sobriquet followed her. A curious triangle we made of it to this very day.

September 24, 1878

If ma friendship for Wyatt became a problem for Kate, the specter of Mattie insinuated itself between us from the moment Kate learned of the love of ma life. She was too worldly to be bothered by the scandalous nature of such a blood bond. Ah made it more personal than that by the daguerreotype Ah held dear to ma heart. Lovely, refined, the picture of femininity, a paragon of virtue, Mattie, everything Kate could never be. Then we drank. Drank too much at the Alhambra that September night. Both of us. Ah was drunk. We quarreled. May have been Mattie again, Ah do not remember. Ah went to our room at Dodge House and fell into bed.

Later. No knowing how long, Ah awakened to pounding at the door. "Go away."

"It's my room too, Doc Holliday. Now open this door, damn you."

"Open it yourself."

"I don't have a key."

"Then make yourself home elsewhere."

"Grrr. . . ."

The door burst from its hinges and crashed to the floor. Ah rolled over in bed. Kate leveled her pistol at me.

"Treat *me* like shit, you son-of-a-bitch. Sorry I ain't her. Never gonna be. Tell you what I will do, though. Send you to kingdom come full of holes. I will."

With that, she fired, narrowly missing me by the width of a hand-span. Ah believe Ah sobered in that moment. Ah leaped out of bed, took the pistol from her hand, and wacked her upside the head with it, knocking her down. Blood seeped from a cut in her scalp.

"Kate, darlin, what have Ah done?"

"Brought me to my senses," she groaned. She cried.

Ah knelt at her side. Held her.

"I might have killed you."

"Ah shall truly treasure the memory of your poor shooting. Here let me help you up." Ah set her on the bed with a towel for her cut. Boots sounded on the stairs. Ah turned to the door and saw Wyatt.

"Doc, someone reported a shot fired. You all right?"

"Accidental discharge, Wyatt. Nothing more."

He lifted his chin over ma shoulder. "Why's Kate bleeding?"

"Bumped my head," Kate said. "Clumsy me."

"What are you going to do about this door?"

"Prop it closed with a chair until morning."

"You sure everything is all right?"

"Just fine. Now go on about protecting the good citizens of Dodge City who may be in need of protection."

Wyatt obliged. By the time Ah had the door temporarily secured, Ah found Kate ready to make matters right between us. And so, we did. For all we may have left wanting of emotional ties, there remained tender union given to express feelings not wholly unrequited. Half a loaf.

As cattle season progressed that summer, the dun haze that greeted our arrival in Dodge made its effect known to ma health. *Cugh, cugh, cugh.* Blood. Ma health worsened. Clothes hung on the bag of bones Ah inhabited for a body. Kate complained Ah drenched the sheets at night with sweat. Summer in a Kansas cow town did not comport with ma condition. She broached our situation one morning.

"Doc, darlin', this place, the heat, the dust, they're gonna kill you."

"The disease," — *cugh, cugh* — "is going to kill me in its own sweet time."

"Perhaps you should consider a sanitorium."

"A pest house? Never."

"People in your condition find relief there. Some are even cured."

"Not John Henry Holliday."

"Ugh! So stubborn. You and your gentrified code of southern societal station."

"Now, now, don't be angry with me. Let me stake us to a little traveling money. Ah am told the hot springs in Las Vegas, New Mexico, relieve those who suffer this disease and do so without the indignity of enduring a house of pestilence."

"Promise?"

"I do."

"I like the sound of that."

Ah have no doubt Kate's concern for ma health was genuine. Ah also suspect her desire to separate me from Wyatt weighed on her judgement. Not long after our discussion, Dodge City's growing appetite for respectability produced new and this time more enforceable ordinances in regard to gambling and prostitution. The ordinances conveniently became effective that fall following the end of the cattle season. The city father's appetite for respectability curiously coinciding with maintaining cowboy "hospitality" through the end of a profitable season. The reformers who advocated for such things were only too pleased to have achieved their purpose. It was in fact time to pick up stakes and move on. The ordinances provided agreeable excuse.

Adobe Hotel
Gallinas Canyon
December 1878

We departed Dodge City that fall. Wyatt saw ma departure for Kate's "big nose" meddling in ma affairs once more. Ah assured him we were leaving out of genuine concern for ma health. True to the sentiment, we were forced to pause our journey for a ten-day respite in Trinidad, Colorado, where Ah suffered the effect of winter mountain air on ma weakened lungs. Trinidad is located along the Santa Fe trail. When I recovered sufficiently to continue our journey, Kate arranged for us to travel by freighter. Thus, Ah was able to complete the journey, lying on ma back in a wagon with no need to sit astride a horse. Kate sat by ma side to see to such comforts as might be made of the primitive circumstances of travel by freight wagon.

On reaching Las Vegas we found the town

suited to our tastes. The gaming action afforded me opportunity as did the fact the area had no offering of dental services. Kate's services of course were in demand wherever men were found. Ah opened ma dental practice in an office on Bridge Street, next door to jeweler William Leonard with whom Ah struck up a friendship over the fact both of us suffered consumption. For all the comity of this beginning, Bill Leonard's and ma stars were destined to cross.

Las Vegas attracted a community of patients suffering consumption for the palliative powers of the hot springs at Gallinas Canyon, six miles north of town. Bill introduced us to the society of sufferers known as the Lungers Club. We found it a sociable circle devoted to making the best of bad circumstances in steaming waters promising relief and possible cure.

We traveled a rough mountain road by buggy to visit the hot springs housed in rough-hewn timber and clapboard bath houses, providing some protection from the elements and a means to retain both heat and steam. This came a mixed blessing. The heat welcome. The sulfur laced steam, stank of rotten eggs. We suffered it for the prospect of relief from the ravages of consumptive disease whilst enjoying convivial company in a society of sufferers.

Taking the waters was done in bath houses segregated for men and for women. Water temperatures varied depending on the location of the spring with the cooler pleasantly warm and the warmest tolerably hot. Food and refreshments were served in an outdoor setting where bathers could take respite from the waters to enjoy conversation and companionship. Bill Leonard introduced us to the regulars who made up the Lungers Club. Kate for her part preferred social gathering to therapeutic bathing, finding the sulfur aroma off-putting. Ah did not care for the smell much either though put up with it for Kate's sake determined to see it through on the off chance it might help. It did not. Any promise of benefit by the hot springs were tempered to me by bitter winter cold.

Within a month of our arrival, the New Mexico territorial legislature enacted a prohibition on gaming. Ah saw it for a tax by another name and continued to run ma bank, for which Ah was regularly cited. Pesky prohibitions against gaming and the carrying of firearms. Infractions of both gave rise to indictment and fines.

Without gaming income, dentistry left me little opportunity. Ah felt prospects called for return to the tables in Dodge. Kate disapproved of the idea out of concern for ma health as one might expect. She refused to accompany me, stating she had her own business to keep her in Las Vegas, though Ah suspect ma reunion with Wyatt had much to do with her refusal to accompany me.

Hotel Glenwood
Glenwood Springs, Colorado
September 1887

Kate arrived with a bowl of soup and half a ham sandwich. Ah had little appetite for even such modest fare. She set it on the bedside table, fluffed ma pillow, and handed me the bowl with a spoon.

"Now be a good boy for once and eat some lunch."

Ah favored her stern admonition with a smile no more than wan. Ah took a spoonful.

"Where were we?"

"Must we?"

"If Ah'm to have an appetite, we must."

"Las Vegas, though your heart set on returning to Dodge."

"And yours did not."

"Nothing to attract me there and nothing good to come of it for you."

"Ah needed money."

"Have we ever not been in need of money?"

"As luck would have it, Dodge worked out for us that time."

"Us?"

"Ah found financial favor in time to return to your side did Ah not?"

9

Dodge City
June 1879

Ma purpose in returning to Dodge was to make as much cash as possible and return to Las Vegas and Kate. Early summer with cattle herds only having just begun to arrive lacked the action needed to accomplish ma purpose. As it happened, opportunity presented itself from a most unlikely source. Ah sat at a table in the Long Branch early one evening, biding ma time shuffling a deck whilst waiting for a game. Bat Masterson appeared at the batwings, glanced around the room, and headed straight for ma table. Curious. What could the Ford County sheriff have need of me for. Ah'd committed no crime.

"Evenin', Doc."

"Bat. Have a seat. Come for a game?"

"Lookin' for men."

"What sort of men?"

"Competent men such as yourself."

"Competent to do what?"

"Secure the assets of the Atchison Topeka & Santa Fe from here to Canon City."

"Secure the assets?"

"AT&SF is in legal dispute with the Denver & Rio Grande over right of way to the Royal Gorge and service to the silver strike in Leadville."

"Seems Ah read something of that in the paper recently. Court decided in favor of the D&RG as Ah recall."

"AT&SF is appealing. They want their property secured pending a decision on their appeal."

"Canon City is a long way from Ford County."

"I'm acting as deputy U.S. marshal."

"How many men you figure to raise?"

"Fifty good ones should do it."

"Pay?"

"Fifty a week and found."

"How many men have signed on?"

"If you're in, I only need forty-nine more."

"Get busy then, suh. You have forty-nine to go."

Three days later we boarded a westbound AT&SF with a posse of such notoriety as ever before assembled. Some Ah knew only

83

by reputation. As a side benefit of the time spent on the train to Canon City and the time whiled away on watch over the AT&SF assets, Ah learned some of the stories of the more notable posse men and padded ma pockets by their affections for cards.

Gunfighter Ben Thompson was chief among the notables. Bat credited the Englishman with saving his life following a shoot-out in Sweetwater Texas. A dispute arose between a cavalry sergeant named King and Bat over the favors of Mollie Brennan, a friend of Kate's as it would turn out and one of Tom Sherman's Seven Jolly Sisters. When King went for his gun, Molly endeavored to intervene, taking a bullet meant for Bat. The bullet passed through her, lodging in Bat's hip as he killed King. When King's comrades in arms sought to avenge King's death and finish Bat, Thompson stepped in guns drawn. Faced with the formidable and lethal reputation of Ben Thompson, the troopers took merit in retreat. Bat was spared, though to walk with a cane for the rest of his life.

Luke Short's speed and skill with a gun belied his diminutive stature. Not a man to be trifled with in the gaming concessions which he oversaw. Wyatt and Bat were both known to call on Luke when the situation called for men who could handle themselves, though much of Luke's reputation lay in the future.

Dirty Dave Rudabaugh spent more of his time on the wrong side of the law than the right. Bat himself arrested Dave the previous year for train robbery. Dirty Dave turned state's evidence on his partners in crime, accounting for his freedom at the time. He wouldn't toe the line for long, riding with William Bonney, better known as Billy the Kid not long after our work in Colorado. Oh and "Dirty Dave?" Well-deserved sobriquet to those downwind of him.

Mysterious Dave Mather, a known associate of Rudabaugh, enjoyed his mysterious reputation. The mystery attending him arose from the absence of arrests and convictions for depredations attributed to him by association with others whose reputations more invested in arrests and convictions. Allowing for Bat himself and ma participation, we presented an assemblage of competent men of notorious reputation, few would choose to face any among us let alone the prospect of all of us joined in common cause.

Bat stationed posse men at each AT&SF watering station and depot along the route to Canon City at the mouth of the Royal Gorge. The D&RG hired Pinkerton to man the heights at the gorge to assure no right of way development could proceed while various lawsuits wound their way through the courts.

Pueblo

Bat, ma-self, and the other notables took possession of the roundhouse at Pueblo. Operation of the line depended on the roundhouse. Secure it and you controlled the line. Secure it we did when Bat broke into a nearby armory belonging to the Colorado state militia by way of requisitioning a six-pound howitzer, shot, and powder, which he deployed in defense of the roundhouse.

With the roundhouse secured, Bat determined to reconnoiter the situation in Canon City. Ah accompanied him and there got ma first glimpse of the gorge they call royal. Carved by the Arkansas River over thousands of years, the gorge passed between thousand-foot sheer cliffs stretching less than a quarter mile. The gorge itself, a narrow defile, scarcely wide enough for a single rail bed. This chasm would become rail gateway to a rich silver strike in Leadville on the west end of the gorge. A daunting feat of human engineering if ever one were to behold would be required to span the defile. Nature rendered it deadly. Silver rendered it worthy of the cost. Cost measured in men, material, and loss of life.

June 10, 1879

A district court in Alamosa ordered the Santa Fe to turn over its Denver & Rio Grande leasehold. The court order instructed sheriffs in the affected areas to oversee return of Denver & Rio Grande property. Thus, with the stroke of its pen, the court pit the legal jurisdictions in support of both parties to the dispute against one another with a deputy U.S. marshal on one side and county sheriffs on the other.

D&RG instructed their men all along the line to call on local sheriffs to move immediately to enforce the court order. At six o'clock on the morning of June 11, sheriffs backed by Denver & Rio Grande gunmen served the court's order on all Santa Fe men stationed along the line. Some fighting took place in West Denver and Colorado Springs. Resistance was short lived.

None of this was known to us in Pueblo. Denver & Rio Grande forces quickly took the depot and water tank. Bat allowed them to have both. We'd make our stand in the roundhouse, relying on the six-pounder if need be. The only vulnerability we could see to the impregnable roundhouse might have come from a dynamite assault. Bat reckoned rightly the roundhouse too valuable to railroad operations for either side to risk such a gambit. No roundhouse, no silver, made for a standoff to our advantage.

Realization the sheriff's posse faced opposition defended by primed artillery occasioned request for a parley. We then learned the rest of the line had been taken, leaving the roundhouse the last holdout. The court's order had yet to be reversed, the certainty of which depended on which side you spoke to.

D&RG next offered a ten-thousand-dollar reward for recovery of the roundhouse. A most generous gesture none of us had expected. Not wanting to be the cause of bloodshed under the circumstances, Bat agreed to surrender the roundhouse. We pocketed the reward money and returned to Dodge.

With ma share of the reward along with ma spring winnings and the pots Ah took from posse men at the gorge, Ah had the stake Ah needed to return to Kate.

■ ■ ■ ■

Hotel Glenwood
Glenwood Springs, Colorado
September 1887

"And so, darlin', all's well that ends well."

"Well enough that time. With all the gun hands you describe, Earp is conspicuous by his absence."

"Regrettably away on other business, though Ah suspect he should have remained in Dodge. Someone was needed to keep the peace there."

Kate gazed off to some middle distant memory.

"Penny for your thoughts?"

"Mollie Brennan. Hadn't thought of her for quite a spell. Sad story."

"Were you good friends?"

"Good as it gets in the trade. I was there that night. The night she died. She paid a price for it."

"Price for what?"

"Tempting the green-eyed monster."

"Jealousy? How so?"

"Billy Thompson, Ben's no account younger brother, owned the Lady Gay. He and Mollie had an on-again and off-again romance that was off at the time. She used

89

Masterson to flaunt him in Billy's face."

"Where did King come in?"

"Just business, though King didn't know it. That's how the row started. She took a bullet meant for Bat. Bat got his second hand. You know the rest of the story. Too bad really."

"How so?"

"If it had been Billy, Mollie might not have felt the need to get in the middle of the fight. She used Bat, and it put him in harm's way."

"Bat's a big boy."

"Didn't have to be that night."

10

Las Vegas
New Mexico Territory

It is said absence makes the heart grow fonder. Ah live with that every day. Her name is Mattie. Absence also caters cupidity. Kate welcomed ma return with the ardor of absence. Ah suspect she also welcomed ma return in health no worse for wear and with unspoken sentiment for having won me away from Wyatt once again. Ah dismissed the stubborn notion of a bone in the barnyard between them.

Thanks to the railroad rivalry between the Atchison Topeka & Santa Fe and Denver & Rio Grande ma return to Dodge found new prosperity. As it happened the AT&SF was about to grace us with prosperity once again for its almost arrival in Las Vegas in the spring of 1879. Ah say almost arrival for the AT&SF tracks missed Las Vegas by best part of a mile, prompting hasty construction of a tent town populated with restaurants, saloons, gaming parlors, and brothels. Dubbed East Las Vegas, locals called it New Town. Such law as Las Vegas had, stopped short of east, a discrepancy of circumstance soon to be filled by those who found opportunity on the edge of those righteous mores of respectability.

Sports followed the railroad to New Town. Some familiar from ma Royal Gorge days included Dirty Dave Rudabaugh, Mysterious Dave Mather, and Josh Webb. Dodge saloonkeeper Hoodoo Brown opened a new watering hole and soon became East Las Vegas's first mayor. With New Town's administration safely in the hands of gaming interests, Ah saw commercial opportunity.

Kate and Ah found Las Vegas an agreeable place and thought to settle there for an extended stay. To that end Ah commissioned construction of The Holliday Saloon a block from the depot. A small clapboard affair, the building afforded sufficient space to house its intended gambling concession and the essential bar. While Las Vegas held itself righteous by ordinances against gaming and other vices, Ah reckoned Hoodoo would have ma back with prosperity certain to flourish.

Sadly, in less than a month, Las Vegas

authorities asserted jurisdiction over New Town. Righteous city fathers could not abide a presence deemed to rival Sodom and Gomorrah within walking distance of their respectable town. Clearly, they lacked the civic sense to appreciate the value of a "dead line" adjacent to a respectable community. That New Town offered alternatives to saloons remaining in Old Town likely contributed to the indignation of the righteous. With their annexed assertion of jurisdiction, Ah found ma-self charged with operating a gambling concession and carrying a concealed firearm. In Dodge these things tended to be annoyances, little more than licensing fees and taxes designed by another name. Nonetheless three hundred dollars in fines nearly equaled the cost of the entire establishment.

July 19, 1879
Mike Gordon got drunk in Las Vegas. He came over to east town looking for trouble. He found it when he started shooting into the dance hall where a girl he fancied worked. While New Town enjoyed the Old Town trappings of respectability, police protection was less certain to be available when timely needed. Such a dangerous situation could not be allowed to persist. Shots

were exchanged in the dead of night. Gordon was found mortally wounded hours later. He died the next morning. A coroner's inquest ruled the matter justifiable homicide by person or persons unknown. Some say Ah killed him. Ah never said Ah did.

October 18, 1879
On a bright sun-soaked Saturday morning Ah ventured into the Plaza in old Las Vegas to attend to some shopping. As Ah went about ma errands a familiar voice called out to me.

"Doc!"

Ah turned. Wyatt Earp. Ah smiled. He was accompanied by his Mattie, brother James, his wife, and stepdaughter.

"Wyatt, what are you doing here?"

"Passing through. On our way to Arizona."

"Arizona, whatever for?"

"Big silver strike around Tombstone. Money to be made there for sure. What are you up to these days?"

"Opened a saloon."

"Still running your faro bank?"

"Ah'd hoped."

"Sore subject?"

"New Mexico law Las Vegas has chosen to enforce."

"Sorry to hear that. No such trouble in

Arizona. Why not come along with us? You could run your bank on some of that silver."

"Ah'd have to talk it over with Kate."

"Still with her, huh. Tell you what, we're camped west of town. Bring her by for supper tonight. Maybe we can talk her into a share of boom town prosperity."

"Ah will see you tonight then."

"Good."

That afternoon Ah broached the subject with Kate.

"Wyatt Earp again. Can we never be shut of that man? Tombstone, no less. If ever there were a match made in heaven for you two, that would be the name for it. Look around, Doc. We've found a good life here. You've said so yourself. Why would you want to run off with the likes of the Earp's for a silver strike that could peter out before we even get there?"

"Now, Kate, be reasonable. Ah'm only asking you to go to supper and hear Wyatt out."

"I *am* being reasonable, Doc. *You're* the one with the wild hair up your ass."

"Nothing wild about making money, Kate, darlin'. Never has been. Ah can't afford the fines to run ma bank here."

"We ain't starvin', are we?"

"We can do better, Kate. All Ah'm asking

is that you listen."

"Not *my* listening worries me. It's *you* listening that leads to trouble."

We listened around the campfire that evening. Tombstone brimmed with opportunity to hear Wyatt tell it. Men with ambition and ability could well find their fortunes there. With disease having all but foreclosed ma practice of dentistry and prohibitions denying ma gaming concession, Ah saw limits to ma future in Las Vegas. Kate for her part remained unconvinced and remained steadfastly opposed to the venture. Ah thought it might separate us when Ah determined to go. She gave up her objection grudgingly without giving up her grudge. We left the following afternoon headed for Prescott where Virgil and Allie lived.

The journey by wagon from Las Vegas to Prescott took a month. Kate and Ah traveled in Wyatt's wagon with Mattie. It made for an awkward time between us. Kate had ample time and reason to polish her grudge on the journey. We had little privacy for conversation. Wyatt and Ah enjoyed each other's company. Kate and Mattie had little in common other than Mattie providing constant reminder of another Mattie she maintained jealous feelings for.

■ ■ ■ ■

Prescott, Arizona
November 1879

Our circumstances changed when we reached Prescott. The Earp brothers went off to assist Virgil and Allie in packing and preparations for the journey to Tombstone. We took room in a hotel and a respite to privacy long overdue.

Prescott charmed Kate. Ah couldn't be sure if it was Prescott's charm or the fact the town was not Wyatt's wagon. Prescott, like so many other towns, got its start with the discovery of gold in the area. Some modest commerce remained in the metal, overshadowed by robust businesses in logging and lumber. Prescott served as territorial capital adding to the town's prestige and prosperity. Ah soon found a gaming concession receptive to ma faro bank and helpful to ma livelihood, which was all the encouragement Kate needed. She began as we climbed into bed at the end of a long and profitable night at ma game.

"Doc, Prescott's a bird in the hand. Who knows what's in the bush down in Tombstone?"

"Are you suggesting we stay here and not

continue on with Wyatt and his brothers?"

"I am. We know what we have here. Tombstone is a roll of the dice."

Ah thought some. Ah knew this was more about her feelings where Wyatt was concerned. She did not like him, plain as that. What's more she resented ma friendship with him. Still there was something to be said for her views on Prescott. Booms often peter out. The territory and town had yet to take on pretensions to respectability such as foreclose opportunities to our professions.

Kate had a point. Prescott offered stability. Should we stay awhile, Tombstone would still be there.

"You make good sense, Kate. Ah believe some time here could be most agreeable to us."

"John Henry Holliday, come here, love. I've got a little something to help you sleep."

And she did. Aw, sweet surrender.

Hotel Glenwood
Glenwood Springs, Colorado
September 1887

As ah came to the close at this point in the story, Kate declared it time for supper. She departed, promising to return directly with something for me. *Cugh, cugh, cugh . . . cugh. . . .* Ah poured ma-self a stout measure. For medicinal purposes, of course. Ah must have dozed as next Ah knew Kate returned with a tray. She fluffed ma pillows and set the tray on ma lap. Ah inspected. A cup of clear broth, a sourdough roll with a pat of butter, green beans, and a few bites of something brown Ah took to be beef.

"Now eat something before we add starvation to your maladies."

Ah took a spoonful of *consommé* as instructed. Kate rocked the bedside chair back against the window casing, half closing her eyes in reflection.

"We were happy there."

"In Prescott?"

"For a time."

"The only thing constant in time is change."

"My, my, aren't *we* profound this evening. Eat some of that beef. You need your strength."

Ah did as told. Just this side of shoe leather. Whatever happened to good steak?

11

Ah broke the news to Wyatt the following afternoon as Ah helped load Virgil's wagon. The wind whipped at the wagon's canvas top, forcing us to shout to be heard.

"You sure, Doc? There're fortunes to be made in Tombstone."

"There's good money to be had here, too. For a time. If Tombstone is as good as you say, it will still be there should Ah later decide to join you."

"It's Kate again, ain't it?"

"Some of it."

"Do not see what you see in that woman. You could easily do better."

"Kate and Ah have an understanding."

"Understanding you let her stand in your way."

Cugh, cugh, cugh. "Understanding a man in ma condition has little to offer. Kate accepts me as Ah am. Few would, you know."

"More than you think if you was to try

and find out."

"We have our differences. We make the best of them."

"If this is the best of them, suit yourself, Doc. I'll write to let you know what you're missin'."

"Ma thanks and good luck." We shook hands, taking our leave. Ah felt the wind at ma back as Ah returned to town.

March 2, 1880
Spring had scarcely breached the new year when righteous misfortune once again cast its shadow over the sporting life. Prescott passed gaming and firearm ordinances detrimental to ma bank. The gaming ordinance required monthly licensing fees with punitive fines for failure to comply. The firearm ordinance, a misguided attempt at civility made maintaining security in a gaming establishment more difficult. We also faced a territorial gaming law scheduled to take effect later that spring. That law would add a territorial gaming license to the cost of running a game. All in all, these policies of civic respectability-imposed tax levies were ruinous to ma business. Ah spoke of it with Kate.

■ ■ ■ ■

Dusty Nugget Saloon

Ah had ma layout set and bank open at the Dusty Nugget early the evening the ordinances passed. Kate came by as she often did. We took a bottle and glasses to ma table awaiting a game. Ah poured. Pale evening light filtered through smudged and streaked window glass, softening tawdry light before the lamps were lit.

"We must enjoy what remains of our time here while we may."

"You talk like we're leavin', Doc."

"Only a matter of time now, darlin', what with the passage of the new gaming ordinances and the territorial law soon to be upon us."

She swirled her glass and tossed off her drink. Ah poured another.

"Times are changin', Doc. Decency laws follow civilization west. You can't run away from it for long. Maybe it's time we find a living on that side of the law. Open a mercantile, a hotel, I don't know."

"You mean settle down."

"I suppose."

"You really ready for that, Kate?" Ah took ma drink and poured another. *Cugh,*

cugh . . . cugh, cugh.

"Am I ready for that? Hell, I don't know. I'm willing to try. Look at you, Doc. You're killin' yourself."

"Ah'm already killed, Kate. The imminence of ma demise is the only matter in doubt."

"Where would you go this time? Let me guess. Tombstone? They have territorial law there too, you know."

"It is a tax unless enforcement is punitive. Enforcement here is about to become punitive. We've seen it before."

"We have seen it before, and we'll keep seein' it until we change our ways. Can't you see that?"

"Can't see why Ah should change ma ways for whatever time Ah have left."

"Can't see or won't see."

She pushed back her chair and left in a huff. Ah poured another drink. She had her point. Ah could see that. Likely for ma own good. Good it might be. Ah didn't have to like it.

Las Vegas, New Mexico
March 1880
With matters unresolved between Kate and me, Ah needed time to think. Unfinished business in Las Vegas provided reason for a

return visit. There would be no month-long plod in a wagon this trip. Ah booked passage on the Star Stage Line. The stage ride gave me time to ponder the possibilities implied by settling down in Prescott or moving on. Tombstone beckoned. Prosperity. Adventure. Where Wyatt was concerned there was always adventure afoot. That was the old tug. It might be old, but all of it kept ma mind off the unavoidable advance of disease. Kate had the inevitability of civil society right. Ah couldn't fight it. Neither could Wyatt or any of us. Still, Ah found the notion of settling down with the horseman for a constant companion repugnant. What of adventure? Ah could not abide what little life might be left to me without it.

Ah had gambling and weapons charges outstanding against me in Las Vegas. Ah paid the fines for which Ah received refund of three hundred dollars in bail. That sum sufficient to settle ma outstanding obligations incurred in construction of the Holliday Saloon.

Plaza Saloon
Old Town
If a man has a past, now and again it is apt to catch up with him. Ah note this on the occasion of ma visit to Las Vegas. Ah cleared

104

up some matters left unfinished there by ma hasty departure. Having accomplished ma purpose, Ah sought refreshment and the pleasure of a game at a favored haunt in Old Town. Ah'd no more than swung through the batwings early one evening two days after ma arrival in town when Ah was confronted by an old antagonist from ma past.

Charlie White and Ah went back to Dodge City days. There we very nearly went to gunplay over a gambling dispute. Bad blood persisted between us until he took to better judgement and left town. As Ah entered the Plaza, Ah was fortunate to spot him at the end of the bar as he spotted me. He went for his gun. Ah bested him with a quick shot. He fell behind the bar. Ah holstered ma gun and left the saloon without waiting to encounter the law.

Ah rode over to New Town convinced Ah'd killed him. Ma reputation in Las Vegas was such, Ah could hear the murder charges being read at the inquest certain to follow. Ah knew Ah could get a fair hearing from Hoodoo Brown. Ah found him in the Holliday Saloon.

"Well, look what the cat dragged in. Doc Holliday himself. Heard you were in town, thought we might see something of you before this. What brings you by?"

"Trouble, Ah'm afraid, Hoodoo."

"When it comes to Doc Holliday, could it be anything else? What is it this time?"

"Ah believe Ah just killed Charlie White."

"You *believe* you did. Tell me about it."

"Ah stopped by the Plaza Saloon over in Old Town. Charlie saw me come in and went for his gun."

"Welcome to Las Vegas."

"We have a . . . history."

"So, it would seem. Sounds like self-defense to me."

"It was, and you'd see it that way. The law in Old Town," Ah shrugged.

"What do you want me to do about it?"

"Arrest me for safe-keeping."

"I can do that, Doc. Don't know if it will stand up to a jurisdiction fight, though."

"Buys some time to organize self-defense witnesses."

"Suit yourself. Right this way."

Ah purchased a bottle to ease the depravations of incarceration. Hoodoo locked me up in his small one cell jail with an office no bigger than the cell. We waited. When no one came looking for me by the next morning, Hoodoo went over to Old Town to make some inquiries. He returned around noon.

"Well, Doc, I got good news and bad news."

"What's the good news?"

"You didn't kill Charlie White."

"Ah saw him go down."

"Grazed him. When he come to, he high-tailed for the next stage out of town. No charges have been filed against you."

"That is good news. Ah guess you can let me out."

Hoodoo retrieved keys from their peg in the office and opened the cell door. Ah stepped out a free man.

"You said you had good news and bad news. What's the bad news?"

Hoodoo lifted a brow. "You ain't as good a shot as you once were."

12

Prescott
August 1880

The stage ride back to Prescott afforded me ample time to think, followed by the pale horse rider. Nothing to be done for it. No telling how long the road before me stretched. Kate favored making a life less inviting to disfavor of the law. Ah could see her point for her. For ma-self, Ah couldn't say. Life, as Ah had expected to live it, was dealt a losing hand by diagnosis of ma disease. Dentistry was now no more than a facade for respectability's sake. Gambling, the only livelihood suited to ma condition. Could Ah turn to some respectable occupation for Kate? Perhaps. In that Ah foresaw the remainder of ma days given to boredom and the death march of disease. All these thoughts roiled ma mind like the dust clouds trailing the *cugh, cugh, cugh . . . cugh, cugh . . .* coach.

Ah returned to Prescott with all these thoughts unresolved to ma satisfaction. Kate knew me well enough. She understood. We did not speak of it until the letter arrived. Ah returned to the hotel after a long night at the tables. Kate awoke as Ah made ready for bed.

"Letter came for you today. It's on the dresser."

"A letter?"

"From Tombstone."

Ah lit the nightstand lamp and sat on the bed to read.

Tombstone
July 1880

Doc,

Hope this finds you well. Tombstone is everything we hoped it to be. Prosperity flows in rivers of silver. Gaming is suited to your bank. No dentist in town. Opportunities abound for you, my friend. Join us. Kate too for all that.

Wyatt

"You going to Tombstone?"

"Thinking about it."

"You hitch your wagon to the Earps, be nothin' but trouble."

"Wyatt's ma friend."

"Wyatt's trouble."

"Ah cannot make a living at gaming here."

"Who says gambling is the only way to make a living."

"It is the only way suited to our tastes and ma condition."

"Leave my tastes out of it. They can change."

"Ah have no interest in changing ma tastes."

"Go then if you must. I'm going to Globe."

"Globe?"

"Globe. I can think, too, you know."

"What do you plan to do in Globe?"

"Not sure yet. Buy a hotel, maybe open a boardinghouse. Something respectable."

"Respectability, the mother's milk of settled down."

"What's wrong with that?"

"For you, darlin', nothing. Ah can see it for you. It is just not the way Ah plan to end ma days."

"Go to Tombstone with them Earp boys, you'll get your day's end."

"Perhaps so. Then again, perhaps Ah shall join you in Globe should Tombstone fail to measure up."

"Measures up to *what*?"

Ah huffed out the lamp to a room still, dark, and chill.

Tombstone
September 1880

Tombstone stood on Goose Flats, a mesa perched atop the richest silver deposits in Arizona Territory. By the time Ah arrived in Tombstone the town had taken on proper social standing. The silver strike tent town was rapidly being replaced by structures built of adobe and wood. The railroad reached nearby Bisbee to serve the area in the spring of that year making all manner of finery, food, and the necessities of civilized life available. Tombstone offered amenities to pleasure the tastes of all from fine art performances at Schieffelin Hall, named for the town founder and wealthy benefactor, to the more prurient tastes of cowboys and miners to be had at the Bird Cage Variety Theater. To be sure rodents, venomous snakes, and insects still bedeviled the citizenry along with a constant quest for potable water, but fine whiskey and superb cuisine could be had at a reasonable price in pleasant surroundings.

Allen Street ran west to east from First to Sixth Streets, serving as a broad main thoroughfare. Fremont Street paralleled

Allen to the north with Tough Nut Street similarly situated to the south. Allen Street boasted the Occidental Saloon and Alhambra Saloon on the north side of the block between Fourth and Fifth Streets. The Oriental Saloon stood on the corner of Fifth and Allen. Ah took a room at Fly's Boardinghouse at Third and Fremont, an easy walk to Allen Street gaming.

Tombstone, like all the boom towns of ma experience, had its share of rough edges. Edges the mostly Republican business interests preferred to have managed. Trouble in Tombstone mostly came courtesy of a faction known as the Cowboys. These small ranchers, rustlers, and stockmen took advantage of the nearby Mexican border to deal in stolen cattle and horse theft, raiding south of the border and running stolen stock to territorial markets north of the border. Men who operated outside the law on one side of the border also found occasion to do so on the other. Stage runs shipping silver made prizes ripe for the taking.

Men like Wyatt Earp and his brothers were drawn into law enforcement by their reputations. Bill Harris knew the Earp brothers from their Dodge City days, having been Chalk Beeson's partner in the Long Branch Saloon. In Tombstone, Harris had part ownership in the gaming concession at Milt Joyce's Oriental Saloon, along with Lou Rickabaugh and Dick Clark. Harris likely convinced his partners to cut Wyatt in on twenty-five percent of the concession, reckoning Wyatt, his brothers, and ma-self to keep a lid on the place. Bill Harris, Ah suspect, also had a word in Virgil's appointment as deputy U.S. marshal for Arizona Territory and Wyatt's employment as a Wells Fargo shotgun messenger and deputy sheriff of Pima County. James and Morgan Earp of less colorful reputations found employment tending bar at a bowling alley on Allen Street in James's case, while Morgan began investing in real estate and mining claims on behalf of himself and his brothers. The mining claim practice involved staking claims in hope of an assay to entice a cash buyer who might actually work the claim.

For ma part, Ah was only too pleased to play the Oriental. From its gala opening, Milt Joyce's Oriental Saloon took Tombstone by storm for its elegance. A stately bar ran the right side of the building back to a stylish private gaming room Joyce leased to concessionaires. The Oriental's rapid rise in popularity soon attracted the envy of competing sporting parlors, whose owners employed miscreant hoodlum and

113

part-time Cowboy associate, Johnny Tyler, to disrupt the Oriental's genteel atmosphere. That is where Ah came in with Wyatt's encouragement. Keeping a lid on Tyler proved a kettle soon coming to boil.

Hotel Glenwood
Glenwood Springs, Colorado
September 1887

Ah yawned. Kate dozed in the chair at ma bedside. She came awake at the pause in ma story.

"A kettle soon coming to boil," she repeated. "Soon coming to a boil? Where the Earp's are concerned the boil never stopped, Doc."

She shook her head in a most I-told-you-so demeanor.

"Good of you to remind me. I own having made ma choices. Some perhaps, not always for the better."

"Some *perhaps*?"

"Ma choices, nonetheless. You made yours as Ah recall. Comfortably situated in Globe not bothered by ma troubles."

"Situated in Globe, alone. Denied the comfort we might have given one another."

"A situation, as Ah recall, of *your* choosing."

"Water passed under the bridge. Let us

speak no more of it this night." She huffed out the lamp.

"Good night, Doc."

13

Oriental Saloon
October 11, 1880

Ah sat at ma game when Tyler came in. He bellied up to the bar and ordered a drink. Wyatt, ever vigilant where Tyler was concerned, stepped up to the bar beside him.

"What can I do for you, Johnny?"

Tyler gave him a surly look. "You? You can leave me alone, Earp."

"Glad to hear that. Guess that means you'll be behavin' yourself tonight, then."

"What's that supposed to mean?"

"Like I said, behave yourself."

"I'll do as I please, and it ain't none of your damn business."

"It is in *my* place. You lookin' for trouble, find it somewhere else."

"You askin' me to leave?"

"I'm tellin' you to."

"Who the hell do you think you are? You ain't packin' no Dodge City star here."

"Don't need one for the likes of you."

"Oh, yeah?"

Tyler took a wild swing Wyatt blocked, twisted Tyler's arm behind his back, grabbed him by the shirt collar, and threw him into the street, much to ma amusement and that of those around me.

Later that evening, Tyler returned while Wyatt was out for supper. Ah noted that he was armed. He looked around before approaching the bartender.

"Where's Earp?"

At that point, Ah decided it best to excuse ma-self from ma game, just as Wyatt returned.

"Mister Tyler," Ah said. "You are aware your presence here is unwelcome." He apprized me with indignation.

"Yeah, Holliday, what are you going to do about it?"

Ah laughed. "Please, suh, you do not wish to further humiliate yourself this evening."

A reddened grimace tipped the next play. He went for his gun as did Ah. Wyatt stayed my hand while Joyce disarmed Tyler. At this point we both found our presence in the Oriental unwelcome. Joyce collected my gun as Tyler and Ah were both shown out to the street. He to go off making empty threats against ma person, me to the Alhambra where Ah composed ma-self over a whiskey. There upon I returned to the Oriental to demand the return of my firearm.

Ah found Joyce behind the bar.

"I told you to get out of here and stay out until you cool down."

"And Ah shall, suh. Ah have only come for the return of ma gun."

"Not tonight."

"But tonight is the point, suh. That man Tyler has threatened me. Ah must be able to defend ma-self."

"Go to your room. That'll defend you well enough for the night."

Ah could see no reasoning with the man on these terms. Still Ah considered being publicly disarmed humiliating and a matter of honor. Ah repaired to ma room to rearm with the Colt Lightening Ah maintained for backup. Returning to the Oriental once more to make ma demand known to Joyce.

Ah did not see the man on entering the saloon. As Ah cast ma eyes about the room in search of him, Ah was struck a blow to the back of the head, knocking me to the floor. Joyce fell upon me, and a scuffle ensued. Noting a gun in his hand, Ah went to ma trigger. The discharge struck Joyce in the hand, disarming him of his gun. With the fight taken out of the man, Ah considered the matter of ma honor settled and departed the saloon with no further incident.

The following day, Joyce filed charges alleging assault with a deadly weapon and attempted murder. City Marshal Fred White soon paid me a visit with a warrant for ma arrest. When witnesses for the prosecution failed to appear at my arraignment, Ah pled guilty to a minor assault charge for which Ah paid a fine and court costs.

November 2, 1880
Johnny Tyler was not the only source of friction opposing Wyatt and his brothers. When it came to law enforcement, politics always played a part. Wyatt aligned himself with Tombstone's influential Republican business leaders who favored his no-nonsense brand of law enforcement. The Cowboy faction in the persons of Ike Clanton and his clan, the McLaury brothers, John Ringo, and Curly Bill Brocius, along with most of the small ranchers and farmers, all aligned with Democrat preferences for law enforcement willing to overlook troubles that mattered little to peace and tranquility in Tombstone. Rustling being a prime example. Matters came to a head with the 1880 election for Pima County Sheriff. Person-

ally, Ah don't consider ma-self political but in these matters as well as others we shall see, ma friendship for Wyatt gave me stake in the outcome.

Incumbent Democrat, Charlie Shibell, faced Republican challenger, Bob Paul, in the race for county sheriff. The office was a political plumb job. Aside from community prominence and a generous salary the sheriff was responsible for tax collection, a portion of which went to the sheriff as incentive to diligence in performing the duties of office. Paul, a Wells Fargo shotgun messenger, had a reputation for strict enforcement of the law owing to a position he held before coming to Tombstone. Democrat interests much preferred the more tolerant Shibell.

John Ringo managed to get himself and Ike Clanton appointed to supervise polling at the heavily Democrat San Simon Valley precinct. As events would unfold, not surprisingly, Shibell emerged the winner by a narrow margin of fewer than fifty votes. Curiously, the Cowboy precinct overseen by Ringo and Clanton went for Shibell by more than one hundred votes, cast on behalf of all fifty eligible voters. In protest, Bob Paul challenged the election result.

Wyatt's place in all this revolved around

the belief Tombstone was about to be hived off Pima County and established as its own county jurisdiction with its own county sheriff, a position Wyatt aspired to. In the months running up to the November election, Wyatt served as a Pima County deputy sheriff, hoping to demonstrate his law enforcement abilities preparatory to a run for sheriff of the expected new county. With the election in dispute, Wyatt resigned the position to work for Bob Paul, making him a loyal Republican certain to be reinstated when the election was lawfully awarded to Paul. Those plans of mice and men took a turn when Shibell appointed Democrat Johnny Behan to replace Wyatt. Wyatt, his brothers, and by association, ma-self all crossed the line by opposition to the violent men of the Cowboy faction.

We did not reckon the import of this adversarial turn at the time, but time would indeed prove the aligning consequential both politically and personally. For ma part, Ah saw the Cowboys as ruffians and petty hoodlums of no particular concern. A misestimation Ah should regret as events would unfold.

January 1881
Where cowboys gathered, trouble was sel-

121

dom far off. Early in the new year, Curly Bill and some of his pals shot up Charleston and Contention, two small towns not far from Tombstone. Neither community employed law enforcement strong enough to stand up to a lawless element in large numbers. The nearest jurisdiction with responsibility to maintain law and order would fall to Pima County where Sheriff Shibell and Deputy Behan had no interest in Cowboys blowing off a little steam.

A few days later a dispute in a Charleston saloon turned to gun play when a hot-headed gambler by the name of O'Rourke, known to me by the handle Johnny Behind-the-Deuce, shot and killed the local blacksmith. O'Rourke was taken into custody by the town constable who, fearing a hanging bee on the part of the popular blacksmith's friends, drove the accused to Tombstone, making him town marshal Ben Sippy's problem. The Charleston mob arrived in Tombstone filled with righteous anger only vigilante justice could appease. They fortified their demands for summary justice with whiskey while adding a few sympathetic locals to their number. The good folk in Tombstone having their own frustrations with Cowboy depredations.

With a mob threatening the jail and

demanding the prisoner, Marshal Sippy called for help. Virgil responded along with Johnny Behan who never missed an opportunity to curry notoriety. Where one Earp went in the way of trouble, you could count on Wyatt and Morgan to throw in. Ah too felt obliged to stand with ma friends — a behavior of loyalty, having become habitual in our Dodge City days. Ben Sippy was no lawman. His hold on the office of city marshal was caught in the throes of coming to an end. Behan could be counted on to gladhand from a safe distance. Thus, it fell to Virgil, Wyatt, Morgan, and me to face the angry mob. Virgil, who wore authority naturally, took charge. A rangy figure, craggy featured with a drooping grey moustache and cool watery eyes. Morg cut the unmistakable baring of an Earp, the like of a more compact Wyatt.

The City Marshal's office and two-cell jail adjoined the Recorder's Court on Fremont Street at Fourth. The mob gathered around the Allen Street saloons a block south. There they continued to fortify themselves with liquid courage until their ire peaked around dusk. They marched up Fourth Street shoulder to shoulder darkened in shadows of gathering gloom. We waited on the boardwalk outside the jail, Sippy and

Behan having withdrawn within to secure the prisoner's safety. Safety all right, theirs in the name of the prisoner. Virgil broke the silence as we watched them come.

"Who do you suppose is leadin' this fandango?"

Wyatt squinted into the fading light. "Looks like Hollis Bunker, the blacksmith's brother."

"Makes sense."

"Why do you ask?" Morg said.

"He's the one we need to convince a hangin' bee ain't the answer."

"Think you can do it?"

"We'll find out soon enough."

Virg cradled a sawed off eight gauge in the crook of his left arm. He let them turn the corner on Allen, giving us line of sight to all of them.

"Far enough. Stop right there."

"Says who?" the blacksmith's burly brother called.

"Virgil Earp says. Marshal Sippy's deputies."

"We come for the prisoner," he said shaking a coil of rope leaving no doubt as to their intentions. "Sombitch killed my brother. Now he's gonna hang."

"Nobody's hangin' without a fair trial."

"Com'on, boys. They cain't hold us all."

Virg discharged one barrel into the air. The blast reverberated off the buildings in the quiet evening air. He leveled the weapon at the crowd. "Take another step, Hollis, and this barrel is for you."

On that Wyatt, Morgan, and Ah all drew.

"He killed my brother."

"For which he will be tried in a court of law. He will not be strung up by a vigilante mob. Think about it, Hollis. Haven't the Bunkers lost enough kin already?"

The shotgun blast weakened the will of the mob. Some began to drift away back down Fourth Street to the safety and comfort of the saloons. When Hollis glanced around, he could see the might of the mob thinning into the night. Others followed his gaze to second thoughts of their own.

"I'll see him swing."

"Justice be done."

And with that, he followed the rest of the crowd back the way they'd come.

Ending the threat afforded Sippy time to spirit O'Rourke out of town, where he might safely await trial in Tucson. Mayor John Clum, editor of the Tombstone Epitaph covered the story, crediting Sippy and Virgil for settling the matter short of violence. Behan, too, came in for more credit than deserved with no mention of those of us who stood shoulder to shoulder with Virg in the face of the worst of the threat. Politics and law enforcement. Law enforcement and politics. Like beauty only to be seen in the eyes of the beholder. The beholder's vision passed on through the prism of the press to a verdict rendered in the court of public opinion. At the time we little appreciated that power of the pen.

14

Oriental Saloon
January 1881

The territorial legislature acted, as most expected they would, taking seven thousand square miles north and east of Fort Huachuca and Benson south to the border, establishing Cochise County. Now it was up to Arizona Territorial Governor John C. Fremont, a Republican, to appoint an interim sheriff to serve until the next election in November of the following year. It was an appointment Wyatt had his heart set on.

Fremont was a legend in the west, much of it made in his own mind. Reputation credited his early explorations following Lewis and Clark with opening the west to settlement. In truth, a politically connected father-in-law set him up for such success as he achieved by the diligent guidance of true frontiersman, Kit Carson. Fremont served as Union general in command of the west during the war of northern aggression, sitting on his pompous ass until Lincoln relieved him of command in favor of the war criminal Hiram Grant who misspelled his way into West Point as Ulysses Simpson Grant. An error U. S. Grant made certain to preserve. Ah digress. All these lofty accomplishments qualified Fremont for a failed Republican run for president, the reward for which had President Rutherford B. Hayes appoint him Arizona Territorial governor. This then was the man Wyatt was to pin his hopes on. We discussed it over drinks at the Oriental one evening not long after the legislature announced its plan.

"Ah read Clum's column in the *Epitaph* this afternoon. Looks like we're on our way to a new county. He allows as how the new sheriff will have plenty on his plate what with outlaws crossing such a long border from both sides and all that rough mountainous country in New Mexico to get lost in."

"Clum's right for once. It'll take a tough experienced man for the job."

"Got anyone in mind?"

"Not a joking matter, Doc. You know I'm the most qualified man for that job."

"That will be up to Governor Fremont to

decide. You know Johnny Behan will have his hat in the ring."

"Behan's got nowhere near my qualifications. Besides, he's a Democrat. Fremont's a Republican."

"And so are you, but that don't necessarily lock it up for you."

"You think Fremont would appoint a Democrat?"

"He might."

"Why would he do that?"

"He's got a Democrat territorial legislature to deal with."

"He's also got a qualified loyal Republican to appoint to the job. He knows I worked my ass off to get Bob Paul a fair shake after the Democrats stole his Pima County election."

"He does know that. He also knows Behan's got powerful Democrat connections. How well does Fremont know you?"

Wyatt shrugged. "By reputation, I guess."

"Ever gone up to Prescott and introduced yourself to him? You know, let him see for himself you want the job. Tell him about your Dodge City days. Let him ask you any questions he may have."

"You really think I need to do that?"

"You can bet Behan's kissed his ass."

"Ain't much into kissin' politician ass."

"Course not. Still, you might give it a try. It *is* how the game is played, you know."

"What makes you so politically savvy all at once?"

"Ah have seen reconstruction."

"Fremont ain't reconstructin' anything."

"Call it construction, if you prefer. Point is, a politician is doing the 'structing and where politicians are concerned, nothing comes off as it seems. Pour you another?"

Tombstone Epitaph
February 10, 1881

John C. Fremont, Republican territorial governor, passed over fellow Republican Wyatt Earp to appoint Democrat Johnny Behan Acting Cochise County Sheriff, tossing a bouquet to the Democrat territorial legislature.

Wyatt was despondent at the news.

"My record as a lawman and a Republican should have counted for something, damn it."

"You say, and Ah might agree, but Behan's a carpetbagger. He knows how the game is played. You didn't play the game."

"Shouldn't have to."

"You may feel that way, Wyatt. You may

130

even be right if the cards were played straight, but you're gambler enough to know too often that's not the way the cards get played."

Hotel Glenwood
Glenwood Springs, Colorado
September 1887
The late afternoon sun at her back cloaked Kate in shadow.

"What's so funny?"

Her shoulders shook as she chuckled to herself. "The great Wyatt Earp. Won't play the game and can't understand why he can't ride his self-indulged reputation wherever he wishes to go."

"Ah did ma best to advise him."

"And rightly so. You just can't tell the man anything. It bites him in the ass in the end. Stand close to him as long as you did, Doc, and you get bit, too."

"A matter of interpretation."

"Interpretation or denial? You go along with the rest of this story. I may not have been there for all of it, but I was there for enough of it to know where all this leads."

15

Oriental Saloon
February 25, 1881

With the cochise County sheriff appointment off the table, Wyatt attended to his
gaming concession. We now faced a Cowboy
faction emboldened by a sheriff in Johnny
Behan willing to look the other way no matter the predations they might undertake.
Wyatt sent for Bat Masterson and Luke
Short to join us in Tombstone, working as
dealers in the Oriental gaming concession.
Two deadly reputations added to our own
had something of the desired effect. Cowboy
visits to the Oriental for a time were moti-
vated more out of curiosity than mischief.
Then again, reputation possessed its own
proclivity to attract trouble.

Charlie Storms was a high stakes gambler,
well known among the sporting crowd in
Tombstone. One evening, not long after Bat
and Luke arrived, he sat in at Luke's faro

bank for a long night. Short was a good banker and did well at Storms's expense over the course of the night. Along toward morning, as Bat arrived for his turn at the tables, a dispute broke out when Storms accused Short of cheating.

"You're drunk, Charlie. Get yourself some coffee and a little shuteye before you go making accusations like that."

Storms rose from his chair. "Why you cheatin' little shit, I've a mind to. . . ."

Bat stepped between them with a leave it be look to Luke. "Now Charlie, my friend, what say we take you off to your room. You get some sleep. You'll see things more clearly when you're sober and rested."

"What business is this of yours, Masterson?"

"Makin' it my business so my friend don't get hurt."

"This little shit? I ain't scared of him."

"You should be. You're the friend I'm looking out for. Now be a good fellow and come along."

Bat took Storms by the elbow and escorted him out of the saloon. Men like Storms often misestimated Short. True to his name, he was not a big man. He was also one of the fastest men with a gun Ah have ever seen, and Ah have seen some of the best.

Trouble appeared put to rest when Bat returned a half-hour later. He and Luke stepped outside for a breath of fresh air. Ah did not see what happened next, but as Bat told it, they'd no more than stepped onto the boardwalk when Storms appeared out of nowhere confronting Luke, gun drawn. Ah heard two shots and bolted to the saloon door, my own gun drawn. Charlie Storms lay dead in the street, his shirt smoldering in muzzle flash. Bat said Luke drew and fired before Storms could get off a shot. Luke's second finished him.

Word of the Storms affair spread through the Cowboy faction like wildfire. Like moths to a match, they came to gawk at those who backed Wyatt Earp's play. They'd come in two or three at a time, belly up to the bar, and watch whoever among us might be playing. Luke Short, Bat Masterson, Wyatt Earp, Doc Holliday — none of them wanted a part of any of us let along two or more. Notoriety did a better job of keeping a lid on the unruly than going to gunplay. You didn't need to.

Reputation kept peace in the Oriental. It didn't put a stop to Cowboy trouble, though.

■ ■ ■ ■

March 15, 1881
The day commenced a series of events destined to cause me no end of grief for some time to come. Ah remember the day quite clearly as a light dusting of snow fell the previous night giving the desert an uncommonly fresh face under a bright morning sky. Ah thought to ride up to the Wells, a short distance north of Tombstone, to pay William Leonard a visit. We first encountered Bill Leonard, recently moved to the area, as a friend from the Las Vegas Lungers Club. Ah rented a horse from the Dunbar Livery as was ma custom for such an outing. Bill and Ah spent a most pleasant day together revisiting fond memories of friends we made taking the hot spring waters. Ah returned to Tombstone that evening in company of the Wells proprietor who delivered a load of drinking water to town. Upon returning the horse to Dunbar's, Ah proceeded to the Alhambra Saloon where Ah took a bite of supper before taking a seat at faro. Ah give this detailed account of ma whereabouts and individuals with whom Ah had contact that day and evening as other events taking place at the

time would render them subject to considerable interest and scrutiny.

Early that evening the Wells Fargo stage departed for its scheduled run from Tombstone to Benson. Beyond the usual accompaniment of passengers, this run carried a Wells Fargo consigned strong box containing twenty-six thousand dollars in currency and coin. Bud Philpot drove with Bob Paul, serving as Wells Fargo shotgun messenger. Paul's Wells Fargo employment became necessary while awaiting a court determined outcome in the fraudulent Pima County Sheriff election, then delayed on appeal. As events were later reported, the stage was ambushed by road agents as it approached Drew's Station north of Contention. Gunfire killed Philpot and one third class passenger riding atop the coach. The robbers were thwarted when Bob Paul returned fire and skillfully drove the frightened and exhausted team past the Drew's Station rest stop and on to Benson. There he reported the robbery attempt by wire to Wells Fargo agent Marshall Williams in Tombstone.

While the robbery attempt failed and the Wells Fargo secured shipment remained in good hands, the company took such matters seriously. Those who would try once might well try again, perhaps with greater success. Williams turned to Virgil Earp in his capacity as deputy U.S. marshal, a choice of jurisdiction both necessary and problematic as we shall presently see. As a practical matter, the robbery occurred in Cochise County clearly in the jurisdiction of Sheriff Johnny Behan. Williams knew better than to expect anything but perfunctory pursuit of bandits likely numbered among Behan's Cowboy constituents. Williams turned to Virgil as deputy U.S. marshal, relying on the fact the stage carried mail, thereby making the attempted robbery a federal offense.

Virgil raised a posse composed of Wyatt, Morgan Earp, and Bat Masterson, who remained in the employ of the Oriental gaming concession as a dealer. Wyatt recounted the events of the evening and ensuing days on which Ah rely for this part of the story.

Williams and his posse departed for Benson at once. Not long after, Behan came by word of the robbery attempt. As events would unfold, Ah came to wonder who called on Behan to investigate a matter where Cowboys were involved. Whatever the circumstance, Behan and Deputy Billy Breakenridge were joined by Frank Leslie to form a second posse.

On reaching Benson, Bob Paul recounted his story and agreed to lead the Earp posse to the scene of the attempted holdup. There by the grey light of dawn they found spent cartridges and sign of the robbers' horses being held before lining out toward the Dragoon Mountains. Three days they followed the trail, turning north along the San Pedro River to Len Redfield's ranch. Many small ranchers like Redfield and his brother Hank were known to do business with Cowboys dealing in rustled Mexican stock. Len Redfield claimed to know nothing of the Benson stage holdup when questioned by Virgil and Wyatt. Morgan, on searching the bunkhouse and barn, came upon Luther King, a known associate of the Cowboy faction, hiding in a hay loft. Under questioning, King admitted holding the robbers' horses and was then placed under arrest. Wyatt, who could be a most persuasive questioner, took up the interrogation.

"So, all you did was hold the horses. Is that right, Luther?"

"Y—Y—Yes, sir."

"Bud Philpot's dead. One of the passengers, too. That's murder, Luther. They hang you for murder."

"I didn't kill nobody. I didn't shoot or

nothin'. All I did was hold the horses."

"If you didn't murder those men, who did?"

"I — I — I don't know, exactly."

"You don't know, exactly."

"No, sir. It was dark. I was busy 'cause them horses was spooked."

"Spooked horse can keep a man busy, even an accessory to murder."

"I ain't no ac— act— ses— sorry to no murder."

"Well, you might not be if you was to tell us who might have done the shootin'."

"I said, I don't know."

"You said you 'don't know, exactly.' You *do* know who was with you, don't you?"

"Ain't sayin'."

"Robber who won't talk ain't much good is he, Virgil?"

"Not much."

"We got two men dead and nobody to accuse but Luther here. I say we string him up now and save the territory the cost of trying him."

"Might's well."

"Morg, fetch a rope."

King looked from Williams to Redfield. "He — he can't do that, can he, Len?"

Redfield shrugged.

"Whose gonna stop him?" Williams said.

"C— C— Crane. Jim Crane. H— Harry Head and Leonard, B— Bill Leonard. They done all the shootin'."

"Now that's more like it. Now where can we find those boys?"

"Said they was headin' to New Mexico."

King's accusation of Leonard's involvement later would lead to wild speculations implicating me with the gang for ma having spent the afternoon in the man's company.

No sooner had King given up the suspects when Johnny Behan rode in with his posse and stepped down. It was the first encounter between acting sheriff and would-be sheriff and a harbinger of things to come.

"What have we here, Marshall?" he said addressing Williams. "I got word of a stage robbery and got here as quick as I could."

"Marshal Earp has arrested one of those involved in the attempted holdup and murders."

"Murders? I did not hear about that."

"Bud Philpot, the driver, and a passenger."

"What brings Earp into this? It's Cochise County jurisdiction."

"Mail robbery is a federal offense, Johnny," Virg said.

"Maybe so. Still, my county. I'll take custody of the prisoner."

"This one says the killers is the ones who got away," Wyatt said.

"What killers?"

"Couple of Cowboys, Crane and Head. 'Nuther fella name of Leonard. According to Luther they're headed for New Mexico. We goin' after 'em?"

"With three days head start, they're long gone out of this jurisdiction."

"Sure, they are, Johnny. Just the way you like 'em. Out of your jurisdiction, 'less of course it happens to be election day."

"What are you sayin', Earp?"

"Wyatt's sayin' we're goin' after 'em," Virg said. "You comin' with us?"

"Burn your own horses, if you like. I'll be taking my prisoner back to Tombstone."

Behan took custody of the prisoner and returned to Tombstone, where King promptly escaped jail. Virgil and his brothers, along with Bob Paul, continued pursuit of the robbers, though they lost their trail in rough New Mexico border country.

King named three as having been part of the gang. By the accounts of Bob Paul and passengers on the stage, the gang numbered as many as eight. Others placed suspicion by association on Ike Clanton and Cowboy associates Frank Stilwell, Pete Spencer, and "Curly Bill" Brocius. Behan chose to see things differently. If Leonard was involved, then so must Ah be. Ah made no secret of ma friendship with Leonard and having visited him the afternoon of robbery attempt. Witnesses could attest to the fact Ah'd been seen at the Wells that day with Leonard. Ah, of course, could point to ma presence in Tombstone at the time of the robbery, but such claims counted little in the rumor mill of public opinion.

Indictment by association served a political convenience for Behan who needed cover for allowing King to escape. Newspapers in Tombstone and Tucson, sympathetic to Behan and having low opinion of ma personal reputation, took up speculation as to ma involvement, fanning the flame of rumor. The *Democrat Nugget* newspaper speculated Ah might have involved ma-self in King's escape, as he could be an important witness against me. Witness to a crime for which Ah had not been charged. It seems Ah was to be tried in the court of public opinion and not merely for attempted robbery. No, no, the charge must include two counts of murder for the gun-handy gambler. All this conveniently diverted attention away from the Cowboys and Behan's look the other way policy where the Clanton and McLaury clans were concerned. It also gave Behan the pleasure of poking at the Earp brothers, Wyatt in particular, for my friendship with them. Behan and Wyatt, having become political adversaries over the office of sheriff, now found themselves at further odds over a woman. A combustible brew if ever there was one.

The woman in question, Josephine Marcus, was a dark-eyed enchantress who came to Tombstone to tread the stage as an actress with a traveling company first booked for a performance at the respectable Schieffelin Hall. Josephine hailed from San Francisco money with appetites not given to Victorian formalities and mores. An opportunist, she saw Johnny Behan for a comfortable station in a more free-wheeling frontier lifestyle. Behan, a philandering ladies man, found the mysterious vixen a prize to parade about his ego. Johnny's problem was he could back up little of what he presented himself to be, soon falling short of Josephine's expectations in all but social station. For her part, she could not help but notice in Wyatt all Johnny lacked. A few batted lashes had Wyatt on the scent.

March 24, 1881
Kate came down from Globe for a visit. Ah confess Ah was much preoccupied by ma

143

ongoing trial in the court of public opinion. The cloud of suspicion hung over ma head alleging Ah played a part in the Benson stage holdup. Rumor raged like a prairie wildfire, no doubt fanned by the very Cowboys who committed the crimes. Some went so far as to say Ah killed Bud Philpot over a gambling dispute. A fanciful allegation for a man Ah scarcely knew and never played with. Kate sensed ma unease. We quarreled. Ah behaved badly. Ah returned to ma room to find her dressed for dinner and a night on the town Ah was not up to.

"I come all the way down here to see you, my love, and what am I shown? A man in a foul mood."

"Ma enemies accuse me of crimes Ah did not commit. Am Ah to be happy about that?"

"Your enemies or Earp enemies?"

"Same difference."

"Doesn't have to be, Doc. Wyatt Earp and his brothers are nothing but trouble. You know it, and I know it."

"Wyatt is ma friend."

"So, you always say. Look where it gets you. Accused of a crime you say you didn't commit."

"You think Ah held up that stage?"

"Some of those rumors you're so upset

about implicate the Earp brothers, too. That wouldn't surprise me."

"Wyatt and Morgan did no such thing any more than I did. It is a malicious attempt to sully our reputations to prevent Wyatt from opposing Behan in the next election." *Cugh . . . cugh, cugh.*

"Even if that is so, look at the state it has got you in. It can't do your health one damn bit of good. It doesn't have to be this way, you know, Doc. Come back to Globe with me. The hotel is doing well enough to keep us. You can get some rest and maybe some relief from what ails you."

"The only thing ails me at the moment is you nagging after ma going to Globe. Ah'm doing fine right where Ah am."

"The hell you are. Plain enough for a blind man to see. Suit yourself, Doc Holliday. You ever get your sense to get shut of Wyatt Earp, you can find me in Globe."

With that, she stormed out, slamming the door to make the windowpane rattle. Don't know where she spent the night. Next morning, she was gone. For all our disagreement, she did have a point. Rumors and speculations as to ma involvement in the Benson stage holdup likely had a tether to Wyatt's political ambitions and Cowboy bad blood when it came to the Earps. Ah had witnesses to ma whereabouts the evening in question. What we lacked was a guilty party to hold responsible for the crime. King was small fry, and even he got away. Crane, Head, and Leonard could clear ma name if they were to be apprehended. An unlikely turn of events on Johnny Behan's watch. Ah took some encouragement from one fact of the situation. As long as the shadow of suspicion hung over Wyatt, it hung over his political ambitions. Ah could count on him to see the capture of the guilty as beneficial to his reputation and law enforcement qualifications. Showing Behan to be weak could strengthen Wyatt's eventual campaign and improve his standing in the eyes of a certain woman.

Hotel Glenwood
Glenwood Springs, Colorado
October 1887
Ah paused, feeling the effects of fatigue. *Cugh, cugh . . . cugh.* Ah brought up bloody phlegm to ma ever-present kerchief.

"Take a nap, love. You need some rest."

"Ah believe you are right, darlin'."

"Course I'm right. Been right more than you were *ever* willing to admit about that man. At least your telling of the story give voice to the truth of it."

"Ah, we, rocked on the horns of a dilemma did we not?"

"You may have. I certainly did not. All I ever wanted was what was best for you. You couldn't bring yourself to see that until now."

"Loyalty is honor. It is to be treasured when found."

"You and your code of honor. Think of all you have sacrificed in the name of that badge."

"Ah do . . . and should Ah need to . . . Ah'd do it all over again."

"Get some sleep, Doc. I'll be back with your supper."

16

Oriental Saloon
April 1881

Ah continued to ply ma trade at cards, the fact grating the sensibilities of Behan crony Milt Joyce, owner of the Oriental Saloon. He came to watch the game Ah sat in on one evening. He watched for a while as Ah took two pots.

"Holliday, why don't you take your game off to detract from the reputation of some other establishment?"

"Hear that, boys?" Ah said to ma playing partners. "The owner doesn't like it when the house loses."

"A couple of pots pale to the damage done the reputation of this establishment when the player is a low-down bandit and murderer."

Ah leapt from ma chair. "That, suh, is salacious rumor likely attributed to liars such as yourself and your Cowboy pals."

"You callin' me a liar, Holliday?"

"Ah believe Ah just did."

He went for his gun. Ah had mine cocked at his chest before he cleared the shoulder rig under his coat. Virg appeared out of nowhere.

"Put up your gun, Doc."

"What about him?"

"Leave it be, Milt."

Joyce withdrew his hand from his coat. Ah holstered ma gun.

"He threatened my life, Virgil. You saw it. I wish to file a complaint."

"Take it to the sheriff. Now, Doc, it might be best if you took your game somewhere else for the evening."

Ah did as Virgil suggested. Joyce filed his complaint. Charges were dropped when Ah paid a fine. With his complaint dismissed, Joyce determined to find another outlet for his anger toward me. Johnny Behan and the as yet unsolved Benson stage holdup beckoned. Ah was already implicated by rumor and inuendo. Joyce need only turn circumstance to his advantage.

It came as no surprise when in May Ah was indicted on two counts of murder and a federal charge of mail robbery for a part Ah did not play in the Benson stage holdup. Ma actual whereabouts at the time of the so-called robbery and murders having been well established by numerous witnesses, my attorney argued successfully to delay further proceedings that June pending the next session of the territorial circuit court in Tombstone. The continuance granted did not lessen ma troubles.

Johnny Behan had a festering problem that summer. Tombstone formed a Safety Committee to reduce crime and violence in town. The committee did so with the full support of Mayor John Clum, publisher of the *Tombstone Epitaph* and backing by the full city council. Both were determined to rid Tombstone and Cochise County of the Cowboy faction. In early June they replaced Tombstone Chief of Police, Ben Sippy, with Virgil Earp. Virgil's brand of tough, no nonsense law enforcement soon had the desired effect on public safety in town, much to the satisfaction of the powers that be. Therein lay Behan's problem.

Behan's loose, look-the-other-way policy toward the Cowboys stood stark by contrast to Virgil's law dogging in town. Behan would stand for reelection in November 1882. A savvy politician, he could see powerful forces likely to back an opponent the likes of Wyatt Earp. The county sheriff's job with its tax collecting fees afforded the sheriff what amounted to a lavish living in a frontier town like Tombstone, prosperity he needed to maintain cohabitation with the exotic and demanding Josephine Marcus. Behan meant to keep the job, his intentions toward the lovely Josephine proved a bit less than honorable.

He remained saddled with the unsolved Benson stage affair, tainted by the escape of the only perpetrator taken into custody. He couldn't turn on the Cowboys. They, along with the small ranchers who made common cause with them, represented the base of his political support. Behan saw one politically convenient response to his public opinion problems. Pin the holdup and murders on me. In the bargain, he'd besmirch Wyatt by association. Ah suspect Behan had a hand in rumors implicating Wyatt and Morgan in the attempted Benson stage robbery and murders. It was the perfect solution to his problem. The question was how? Rumor and speculation, no matter how rampant, gave no cause for criminal charges. He got his opportunity gift wrapped when Kate came down from Globe to celebrate Independence Day.

■ ■ ■ ■

July 4, 1881

Ah regretted ma bad behavior toward Kate on her last visit. She surely did not deserve it. It was ma preoccupation with ma troubles set us off. Ah wrote, inviting her to Tombstone for the Independence Day celebrations. Ma good intentions proved one of those paving stones found on the path to perdition. She arrived early afternoon by stage. We set about celebrating our reunion over drinks that carried us into the evening. By the time we thought to retire to our concupiscent needs, we were both quite drunk. Ah do not now remember how Wyatt's name came up or how the row started, only that it did. We picked up where we left off back in the spring with Kate raging the only troubles Ah ever had short of ma disease were wound up with the Earps. Ah had no patience with her constant criticisms of ma friends and said as much, quite colorfully, Ah'm afraid. She stormed out. Ah ordered another drink, only to worsen ma troubles.

She headed for the Oriental Saloon in a raging drunk. There she encountered Milt Joyce. Joyce bought her a drink, sent for

Johnny Behan, and listened to her tales of woe. One cannot know what was said over that drink and likely several more. Behan and Joyce made the Benson stage holdup and ma part in it the subject of conversation. Given Kate's state of mind and inebriated condition, she likely gave vent to her speculations about the Earps and ma involvement in the holdup. Despite the late hour, it was all they needed to take her before Justice Spicer for questioning. She later signed an affidavit stating Ah had confessed to taking part in the holdup and killing both driver and passenger. Awakened from a sound sleep, a disheveled Justice Spicer issued a warrant for ma arrest before returning to bed.

July 5
Behan met me on the boardinghouse boardwalk as Ah made ma way to breakfast around midday.

"You're under arrest, Holliday."

"Excuse me?"

"You heard me. You're under arrest."

"On what charge?"

"Attempted robbery of the Benson stage and the murder of Bud Philpot, driver, and Harley Hopper, passenger."

"That old canard? You cannot be serious,

153

Johnny. My whereabouts at the time of that holdup have been well established."

"I have an affidavit says you confessed to your part in the holdup and murders."

"Ah confessed? Who would say such a thing?"

"Kate Elder signed the statement. Now, come along."

It didn't take long for Wyatt to get word of ma incarceration. He came to the jail directly.

"Johnny, I hear you have Doc locked up. What's the charge?"

"Robbery and murder."

"Robbery and murder? Just exactly what robbery and what murder?"

"Why, the Benson stage holdup and the murders of Bud Philpot and the passenger."

"And what makes you think Doc had anything to do with that?"

"A signed affidavit attesting to his confession."

"Doc confessed?"

"To the attestant."

"Attestant who?"

"Kate Elder."

"Let me see Doc."

"Hand over your gun."

Behan opened the cell block. "You have a visitor, Holliday. Let me know when you're done." He closed and locked the cell block.

"What's all this shit about you confessing to the Benson holdup and murders?"

"Good afternoon, Wyatt. Thank you for coming. Kate and Ah . . . well, we quarreled."

"And for that you confessed to crimes you didn't commit?"

"Ah confessed to no such thing. We were both angry and drunk. Kate stormed off. Ah went to bed. This morning Behan came for me with a warrant for ma arrest. He claims Kate signed an affidavit Ah confessed to the holdup and murders."

"Yeah, I know all that. Let me see what can be done about it. All right, Behan, we're finished."

What could be done was to have Virgil arrest Kate for drunk and disorderly conduct and confine her to a room at the Cosmopolitan Hotel where she could sober up and reflect on what she had done. Sobriety came with remorse.

17

Sobered, Kate determined to do the right thing. Virgil ordered her release. She went to the Oriental to see Joyce.

"Morning, Kate. Come for an eyeopener?"

"I've come to correct that paper I signed. Doc did *not* confess to the holdup or the killin's. We fought. I was mad and drunk. You and Behan put all those thoughts in my head."

"Now, Kate, come along over to this table and let's have a little talk. There, have a seat." He held the chair. "If you'll recall, you said yourself you thought Doc was involved because of the Earps."

"I may have said something like that, but Doc never said he done it. Like I said, I was mad, and I was drunk. I'm going over to Justice Spicer and take back what I said."

"Here, let's have a drink and talk this over."

Joyce went to the bar for a bottle and glasses. He told the bartender to send the swamper for Sheriff Behan, then returned to the table and poured. "You're right, you know."

"Right about what?"

"Doc's problems are caused by those Earp boys."

"You know that, and I know that." She tossed off her drink. "No tellin' Doc that."

"Here, let me top that up for you."

By the time Behan arrived, Kate was well on her way.

"You sent for me, Milt."

"Kate says she's going to Justice Spicer to recant her testimony. We can't have that now, can we?"

"No, sir. By the look of it, I'd say she's drunk."

"Disorderly, too."

"My thoughts exactly."

Behan arrested Kate on drunk and disorderly charges and confined her to a room at the Cowboy-friendly Grand Hotel, this time under county jurisdiction.

All the while this went on Ah remained confined in the Cochise County jail. Bars shadowed the cell floor in late afternoon sun as Behan assured me Kate was safely under protective custody.

"What the hell does she need protective custody for?"

"Protect her from the likes of you and the Earps. She *is* our star witness, you know."

"Witness to what?"

"Your confession to the Benson stage holdup and two cold-blooded murders, of course."

"Ah have never given any such confession."

"We have Kate's word on it."

"The word of a drunk."

"You say. She says you confessed. It will be up to a jury to decide the truth of her testimony."

Cochise County Jail
July 7

Wyatt entered Behan's office shortly before Ah was to be subjected to yet another jail fare lunch. Johnny, ever the cordial gentleman, greeted his arrival with all the warmth of a frosty winter morning.

"What do you want, Earp?"

"Doc's release."

"On what account?"

"Justice Spicer set bail. It's been posted. Here's the receipt."

"Five thousand dollars. You posted five thousand dollars for the release of this bandit, murderer, and degenerate lunger."

"*Alleged* bandit and murderer. We both know that charge is bullshit, Johnny. Now open the cell and let him out."

Mumbling under his breath, Behan retrieved the keys from their peg on the wall. He opened the cell door.

"I'll keep it warm for you, Holliday. You'll be back."

Ah ignored him. "Thank you, Wyatt. Don't know how you managed it, but let me buy you lunch." Ah waited for Behan to return possessions confiscated on ma arrest. He did so, handing over ma pistol at the last.

"Can't believe I'm arming a criminal."

"Fortunate for you, Johnny, Ah am not the criminal you accuse me of." Ah led Wyatt out to the boardwalk. "Alhambra?"

He nodded.

Fly's Boardinghouse
July 8
Drunk and disorderly only entitles a person to so much protective custody. Forced to release Kate, she made good on her promise to do the right thing and recanted her statement before Justice Spicer. She came by

Fly's to tell me and pick up some of her things she'd left there. Ah should have been more appreciative of her honesty, but both of us bore a distemper not soon soothed over.

"How could you do it? The rumors were bad enough without you throwing a lit cigar on dry prairie grass before a high wind."

"I was drunk, and I was pissed. As to drunk, we both were. You own the pissed part. Joyce is a snake. He put me up to it. Behan was only too happy to take advantage."

"But you thought Ah did it."

"Rumors implicating you implicated the Earps. Wherever they are, you're sure to be close by. What was I supposed to think?"

"Not the worst."

"Where the Earps are concerned, it's always the worst for you, Doc. You're just too blind, pigheaded, and closed-minded to see it."

"The Hell! Blind, pigheaded, and stupid is getting a man charged with murder over rumors. If Ah weren't a gentleman, Ah'd slap some sense into you."

"Don't you dare, Doc Holliday." She fished in her purse. "Damn. Behan's still got my gun. If I had it, I'd shoot you dead here and now."

"Good you don't have it. You'd have about as much chance of a fair murder trial in this town as the one you set me up for."

"Set you up. I'll set you up. I don't have it, but I know where to get it."

The door slam rattled the window glass. Ah cracked a half a smile.

Tombstone Police Station

Ah found Virgil at his desk.

"Doc. Heard Wyatt made your bail. What brings you here?"

"Kate."

"Now what? She make another statement?"

"You could say if threatening to kill me is a statement. She's gone looking for her gun. Behan's still got it. If she tells him what she wants it for, he'll likely load it for her."

"What do you want me to do?"

"Have somebody keep an eye on ma back until she cools off or makes a play."

Kate accosted me on ma way back to Fly's.

"There you are, John Henry Holliday!" She reached Fremont from Fourth Street. Turning west, she groped in her handbag, presumably for her gun.

Ah turned back to observe, amused to see Virgil cross Fremont behind her quickening

161

his stride. He reached her as she pulled a pepperbox derringer from her purse.

"Now, Kate, best you let me have that before you hurt someone." He took the gun.

"Hurt someone! I plan to kill the son-of-a-bitch."

"So, it seems. It also seems you've been drinking again. Let's see. Assault with a deadly weapon, intent to kill, drunk and disorderly, I'm afraid I shall have to lock you up for your own good."

"My good. You mean *his* good. There you go again, Doc. The Earp cause of your problems savin' your sorry ass from righteous retribution."

"Kate, darlin', you know you truly mean me no harm."

"Hell, I don't. This goon hadn't taken my gun I'd a shown you sure."

"I'll lock her up till she simmers down, Doc."

"Much obliged."

" 'Much obliged,' he says. Damn straight you're obliged. Obliged to have me arrested again. Third time this visit. And all that after I let you off the hook."

Virgil once again locked her up in the Cosmopolitan Hotel. Though Ah did not press charges, her behavior compromised any standing her accusations may have had.

Investigation by District Attorney Littleton Price found no evidence substantiating Behan's charges of robbery and murder. Kate, having recanted the affidavit, further tainted any credibility she may have had by her public behavior and arrest record. Justice Spicer subsequently dismissed the charges against me July 9. Released from confinement, Kate returned to Globe without further incident.

Hotel Glenwood
Glenwood Springs, Colorado
October 1887

The bedside lamp flickered light and shadow up the wall before fading in darkness near the ceiling. Ah rested ma eyes. Kate rocked, silent in the bedside chair.

"I've tried not to think about that," she said at length. "Not one of the better chapters in our . . . our time together."

"Would you have?"

"Would I have what?"

"Killed me?"

She thought. Ah braced ma-self.

"Likely so, had Earp not intervened. Then I probably would have regretted it."

"Ah take comfort in that."

"You should. I'm here, after all."

"After all. All covers a lot where you and

163

Ah have come from."

"Does. Should never have let Joyce and Behan talk me into signing a paper against you. Whiskey and anger make a bad brew."

"We both had a share in that."

"Only one of us come to the brink of murder for it."

"Ah could forgive you for that. It was only you thought me guilty of those crimes that pained me."

"It was the Earps stickin' in my craw."

"Ah shall never understand such antipathy toward ma friends."

"I understand it. They didn't like me, starting with Wyatt. I didn't like them. That was old Dodge days before you arrived in my life the second time. And then. . . ." She paused again. Lost in some far-off thought. "And then Wyatt come between us." She glanced at the watch pinned to her bodice. "It's late, Doc. Get some rest."

She fluffed ma pillow, huffed out the lamp, framed a silhouette in the hall lit doorway, and was gone with a click of the latch. Ah stared into the darkness. *Cugh, cugh.*

The rider drew nigh.

18

One would hope the dismissal of all charges would put an end to ma troubles in the matter of the Benson stage robbery and murders. One could hope, but the court of public opinion remained much in session, likely owing to a desperate Johnny Behan, whose *coup de gras,* resolving of the unsolved crimes, collapsed in the sworn blathering of a scornful drunken woman. Ah remained in need of clearing ma name if such were ever possible.

Where Ah saw need to clear ma name, Wyatt saw opportunity favorable to his political ambitions and Behan's inability to bring the Benson stage outlaws to justice. Wells Fargo guaranteed shipments entrusted to them. Should any loss occur, the company made good the loss to the shipper. This created monetary risk to Wells Fargo to go along with reputation risk damaging to the company should any loss be incurred. Even though the Benson stage affair produced no loss, Wells Fargo wanted the murderers brought to justice, so much so the company offered twelve hundred dollar rewards for Bill Leonard, Harry Head, and Jim Crane. Wyatt devised a plan to draw Leonard, Head, and Crane into a trap, with the promise of another tempting Wells Fargo shipment.

He secretly approached Ike Clanton, Frank McLaury, and Joe Hill offering the reward money, all $3,600 of it, to them if they passed word of a lucrative Wells Fargo shipment to Leonard, Head, and Crane. He reasoned the *desperados* would take bait offered by trusted Cowboy pals. Ike, Frank, and Joe accepted Wyatt's offer of the reward money. The plan failed for reasons of self-interest and preservation when Hill learned Leonard and Head were already dead. That left only Jim Crane to give Ike Clanton a case of itchy palms where the offer of reward remained.

Throughout the summer of 1881, the Cowboys continued to ply their rustling trade, raiding across the border into Mexico to steal horses and cattle. The business became so lucrative, competing factions arose, leading to armed confrontations between rival gangs. Instability along the border found its way to federal and territorial authorities, leading to the offering of rewards for certain of those involved. One among them, Jim Crane, the last surviving named participant in the Benson robbery and killings and a man whose testimony might finally clear ma name.

The Cowboy faction was a loosely knit confederation of small-time ranchers, rustlers, and outlaws plying their illicit trades freely along the wide-open reaches of the Mexican border. Loose confederation or not, the Cowboys had numbers — the Clantons and McLaurys among them. Both the Clanton and McLaury clans regularly provided business outlets for Cowboy ill-gotten gains in stolen horses and cattle. Newman Haynes, "Old Man" Clanton, patriarch to the Clanton clan ranched rustled cattle with sons Ike, Billy, and Phin. Ike, the oldest, was a thick set dapper dandy, all bravado with nothing to back it up. Billy Clanton combined wild with reckless, a penchant for trouble. Young Phin tagged along with his brothers.

The McLaury brothers, Frank and younger brother Tom, also ran a small-time ranch dealing in rustled horses and cattle. Frank had the look of a well-made man ladies could love despite his diminutive stature. Tom, slightly smaller than his brother, gave a youthful appearance easily misestimated for his violent short fuse.

The Cowboys included such notable rustlers, outlaws, and gunmen as Johnny Ringo, Curly Bill Brocius, Frank Stilwell, Pony Deal, and a host of troublemakers who drifted in and out of the territory. Ringo came to Arizona a killer with a fondness for whiskey belied by the strait-laced look of banker. Curly Bill came by his sobriquet courtesy of a full head of curls. Killer, outlaw, and rustler made Curly Bill fit Cowboy company. Frank Stilwell had an arrogance about him to brook no question. Still questions abounded, including stage robbery and murder. Pony Deal came to Tombstone by way of the Lincoln County war with a taste for murder, stage robbery, and rustling. What more could be said for a Cowboy?

As summer wore on, tension between the Earps and the Cowboys continued to mount. Hostilities came naturally to Earp brothers whose allegiance to law and order put them in direct conflict with Cowboy interests. Wyatt made no secret of his ambition to oppose Behan in a run for sheriff in the next election. In Behan, the Cowboys had a pliant lawman more interested in the trappings and currencies of office than upholding the law. One back served to scratch the other.

A stage robbery in Pima County cast suspicion on Pony Deal and Sherman McMasters. McMasters, a former Texas Ranger, likely found himself keeping the wrong kind of company after arriving in Arizona. Pima County Sheriff Bob Paul wired Virgil to arrest McMasters, who was known to frequent Tombstone. McMasters escaped when he was warned by Johnny Ringo, but the incident convinced Frank McLaury, if he needed further convincing, the Earps were the Cowboy's mortal enemies. For all this, bad blood between Wyatt and Johnny Behan would only worsen. Beside Behan's political affinity for the Cowboys, he was thought to have troubles at home, brought on in no small measure by Josephine having taken romantic notice of Wyatt.

Romantic notice might have been a trifle understated. Ah believe the heat of her notice not only caused Behan problems at home, the "affection infection" soon spread to Wyatt and Mattie who retreated to her comforts in laudanum. It may have been best for all concerned when Josephine announced her intention to return to San

169

Francisco from whence she had come. Best for all save Wyatt, whom she made certain to know where to find her.

Oriental Saloon
August 1881

Late that summer, Ike approached Wyatt with questions later to prove material to events Ah should take a most personal interest in. He took Wyatt aside one evening for a private conversation, notable for the extraordinary nature of such a meeting. Ah noticed he was cautious to know who was present that night. As matters unfolded, Ah suspect his caution assured himself none of his Cowboy associates were there to observe his conversation with Wyatt. They took a back corner table.

"What's on your mind, Ike?"

"You still willin' to pay the Wells Fargo reward for Jim Crane?"

"I am. You willin' to give him up?"

"Maybe."

"Maybe?"

"If Wells Fargo is payin' the reward dead or alive."

"Don't know the answer to that. Why do you ask?"

"I know you, Earp, and I know Crane. He's as likely to be taken dead as alive. I'm takin' a risk, givin' him up. I ain't doin' it without gettin' paid."

Wyatt shrugged. "I can ask Marshall Williams. He may not know, but he can sure find out."

"Find out. Don't let him know why you're askin'. Wrong people hear about this, I'm good as dead."

"Your secret is safe with me, Ike. I'm after Crane. Give me a couple of days."

Ike nodded and left. Ah approached Wyatt.

"What was that all about?"

"Nothin'. Just Ike bein' Ike."

That's all Ah got of it. Ah proceeded to forget about it and thought nothing of it when Ike showed up again two nights later for another chat at the same corner table.

"What did Williams have to say?"

"He didn't know. Had to wire the company."

"And?"

Wyatt handed over a telegram. Ike read. "Satisfied?"

Ike handed the telegram back. "That'll do."

"Thought it might. Now what about Crane?"

"We got a deal?"

"We got a deal."

"Crane and some of the boys been workin'

south of the border. Pa's been buyin'. He's expectin' another herd sometime in the next week or so."

"You know where?"

"Not exactly. They find a spot north of the border, like a draw where they can hold 'em long enough to fix any brands need fixin'."

"Come see me when it's done."

"Count on it."

Next ah knew, Virgil was raising a posse to go after rustlers who'd been seen delivering cattle to Old Man Clanton's ranch. Ah thought it odd for Virgil to step into Behan's jurisdiction on a civil matter such as rustling where a U.S. marshal had no reason to intervene. When Wyatt told me Jim Crane was said to be numbered among the rustlers, Ah thought Virgil's actions perfectly suited to ma purposes. Certain capturing Cane must clear ma name, Ah was only too pleased to join Wyatt, Morgan, and Warren Earp as members of Virgil's posse.

Old Man Clanton's ranch sat on the Arizona and New Mexico border with Mexico. Finding men in such an expanse of rough country is a daunting task in the best of circumstances. Wyatt being Wyatt devised an ingenious plan. We rode south from Bisbee, swinging east just north of the border. Ah pulled up stirrup to stirrup with Wyatt.

"Ah thought you said Crane was seen at Old Man Clanton's ranch."

"I did."

"Then what are we doing here?"

"Followin' the border through Clanton's ranch."

"You figure to find Crane and his Cowboys riding in open country?"

"Not Crane and his men. Cattle."

"Ah don't understand."

"We're lookin' for cattle sign. Hard to hide a herd of cattle coming across the border. We cut their trail and follow it to wherever they're holding the herd."

The stretch of border we rode covered some fifty miles. We rode an easy tracking pace, crossing no trail the first day out. Ah understood what Wyatt told me of his plan. Still, it struck me a roundabout way to track a man known to be in Clanton's company. Around the campfire that first starlit night Ah raised the question once more over a cup of coffee, fortified against the chill with good Kentucky whiskey.

"You sure about this, Wyatt?"

"Sure about what?"

"Finding Crane out here. Seems like a lot of saddle sore for knowing him to be about with Old Man Clanton."

"Clanton's no easier to find than Crane. Cattle's likely to find both of them."

Ah shook ma head.

"Relax, Doc," Morg said. "The man knows what he's doing."

"Don't doubt that. Ah just don't understand the logic."

"Neither do I. It may be we don't have all the information Wyatt has."

At that, Ah knew there to be something more in play here. Something about which Wyatt wasn't talking.

Midmorning the following day, our search was rewarded. Trail sign came up across the border, lining out northeast into hill country. We followed the trail to a canyon holding the herd in an area poetically known as the Devil's Kitchen. There in the purple shadows of early evening we observed Old Man Clanton and a Cowboy crew encamped with their stolen herd. Ah spotted Jim Crane among the Cowboys. It lifted ma spirits. The prospect of clearing ma name rested before ma very eyes.

We made cold camp, getting some rest to the gray light of predawn. Wyatt divided us. He sent Morg and Warren up the west wall of the canyon mouth — Morg to high ground with Warren to hold the mouth.

Wyatt and Ah took the east wall — Wyatt the high ground with me at the mouth. We took our positions to await early dawn light. The canyon lay shrouded in dark shadow. Little stirred more than the lowing of cattle. As dawn broke, and the camp below began to stir, sun climbed over the east canyon wall, blinding those below to the presence of those above. Wyatt broke the stillness.

"Clanton. Throw down your guns. You're under arrest."

All hope of a peaceful outcome ended on Wyatt's command as flashes of gunfire and powder smoke bloomed out of the shadows below. We returned fire to deadly effect with the advantage of high ground and sun-lighted targets. Blinded by the disadvantage of nature, the Cowboys recognized their plight. A few made for their horses. Warren and I, holding lower positions on the canyon wall, climbed down to deny the opportunity of escape. In this we were mostly success-ful, though exposed by the action, Warren and I each sustained bullet wounds to the leg. One Cowboy escaped on horseback. Five died, including Old Man Clanton and Crane, the last hope to clear ma name.

Old Man Clanton's death would salt a wound about to be opened. Crane's death foreclosed the chance to rid ma-self of the persistent Benson stage cloud of suspicion. There was no truth to the rumors, court proceedings having established ma innocence. Still, the whispers persisted, if only to cover for Behan's incompetence. Ah resigned ma-self to ma fate until circumstances might vindicate me beyond question.

19

September 8, 1881

The Tombstone to Bisbee stage was held up once again, this time successfully with the bandits making off with the Wells Fargo strong box. Wells Fargo agent Marshall Williams led a posse including Behan Deputy Billy Breakenridge along with Wyatt and Morgan Earp. They tracked the outlaws and arrested Frank Stilwell and Pete Spencer. With little more than circumstantial evidence against the pair and the aid of witnesses who swore the two were elsewhere at the time of the robbery, charges were dismissed. Still, the incident played into Wyatt's ambitions to defeat Behan in the fall election of 1882. Stilwell occasionally served as a Behan deputy, further sullying the sheriff's reputation for going easy where Cowboys were concerned.

Kate arrived from Globe within days of the robbery. She came partly of affection and partly of necessity, owing to a fire damaging her boardinghouse. Still, Ah was happy to see her. Without speaking of it, we both avoided any mention of Wyatt. It served us well enough in preserving equanimity in our relations. Ah suggested a change of scenery might do us both good, mentioning the Fiesta of San Augustine about to commence in Tucson. Fiesta, even one given in the name of a saint, promised a good time.

We departed by stage the end of September.

Tucson

We spent the best part of a month in the most pleasant of pursuits. Ah would gamble most evenings with Kate at ma side. We retired in the early hours before dawn to sate our appetites and sleep past noon. Afternoons began with breakfast followed by some activity chosen for the day. Fiesta events or a drive in the country among our choices. We dined in the evening before heading to the tables to begin the cycle of daily life all over again. Remarkably, we never fought. Ah remarked on it early one morning in the echoes of carnal bliss preceding the twilight of sleep.

"We have gotten on quite well on this trip,

have we not?"

"Of course, we have. We've not gone near the subjects that bring us to fight. You have not spoken of that man, and I have made no encouragement to a normal life, though these weeks may be as close to normal as we have yet to enjoy."

"That simple?"

"That simple."

"Who knew?"

"I did. I've come to accept matters as they are, Doc. I shall never have the life I desire from you, and I shall never pry you free of your . . . friend."

"You make it sound so one sided."

"If it sounds one sided, it is because it is one sided."

Ah thought for a time. "Ah'm sorry for that."

"Please, Doc, if you were sorry, you might be tempted to change things. I understand that is not going to happen. I accept it. We are about good times. No more than that, and that must be enough."

"Good times?"

"Good times."

She rolled into ma arms.

Tuesday, October 25, 1881
Ah was having a good run bucking the tiger

179

early of an evening in late October. Kate sat at ma side, which was her custom. Between draws, Ah laid ma bets and took a swallow of ma whiskey. Ah felt Kate stiffen as though a chill breeze had blown through a warm autumn evening. Ah glanced around the room to see what might be amiss. Morgan Earp caught ma eye standing beside the batwings. He motioned to me.

"Watch ma bets here will you, Kate."

She clenched her jaw by way of reply as Ah rose.

"Morg, what brings you to Tucson?"

"We need you in Tombstone tomorrow, Doc."

"Tomorrow?"

"Tomorrow."

"That urgent?"

"Would I be here if it weren't?"

"How we going to get there?"

"There's a freight train leaving for Benson in an hour. Wyatt's having a buckboard meet us there."

"Let me cash out. Damn shame for the run Ah'm on." Ah returned to the table to cash out.

"What's he doing here?"

"Some kind of trouble. Ah'm wanted in Tombstone tomorrow."

"Tomorrow?"

"Afraid so. Kate, love, you best stay here. I'll come for you as soon as I am able."

"I'm coming with you."

"There may be trouble."

"Where the Earps are concerned, there's always trouble. I've seen trouble before."

"We're traveling rough."

"If you can travel rough, I can travel rough."

Ah glanced at Morg. "What am I to do with her?"

Morg winked. "Travel rough."

Morg made good his promise of rough travel. The freight took us aboard an unused cattle car. The car, unused on this run, most certainly used on some recent run, previous passengers having left considerable sign of their passage. Kate stood the whole way to Benson, holding a perfumed kerchief to her nose. Morg was close mouthed about the nature of our errand. He deferred ma questions to Wyatt.

The buckboard ride from Benson to Tombstone provided open air relief to the discomforts of a cattle roughened road. Wooden seats, stiff springs, and a rutted road lighted by a sliver of moon and pale starlight lurched and jounced along a road roughened by other means. Kate dozed at ma shoulder in spite of it all. We were weary travelers by the time the lights of Tombstone winked against the dark horizon. At length we clattered into town. Ah directed our driver to Fly's.

Tombstone
10 P.M.
Ah checked Kate in at Fly's Boardinghouse and left for the Alhambra with Morgan. Wyatt awaited us there. Ah could feel tension the moment Ah laid eyes on him, crossing the saloon to a back corner table.

"Doc."

Ah pulled up a chair. "Wyatt. What is so all fired urgent Ah must be taken from a hot run at the tiger to ride a manure wagon through the night to get here?"

"Trouble — and according to Ike Clanton, you're the cause of it."

"Ike Clanton? Ah have had nothing to do with the man."

"Ike claims you told him you knew about the secret deal I had with him to turn over Jim Crane."

"What secret deal? Ah know of no such secret deal. How could Ah have told that overstuffed bag of bovine breeze something of which Ah knew nothing about?"

"Didn't think you did. Just had to hear it from you."

"What secret deal gives Ike Clanton cause for trouble?"

"Ike told me where to find Crane in return for the Wells Fargo reward money. He's angry Old Man Clanton was killed in the gunfight."

"As Ah recall, a gunfight the old man started."

"Such things matter little to Ike. He's afraid his Cowboy pals will find out he betrayed one of their own."

"Selling out one's friends is a sign of low character. It would serve him right if they were to find out. Perhaps Ah should oblige the son-of-a-bitch."

"Don't do it, Doc. Sure as hell it would splash more mud on us. Ike's all bluff and no real threat. Curly Bill, Ringo, some of them others is a different story."

"So, what is to be done?"

"For now, watch your back where Ike is concerned."

"Ah should rather have ma satisfaction of the liar."

"Save your satisfaction. We may need it later."

With the matter settled between us, Ah took to the faro tables hoping to catch the same tiger by the tail as the one Ah left in Tucson. Unfortunately, the Alhambra tiger had a different run of fortune in mind. Ah played for a few hours until hunger reminded me Ah neglected eating over the suddenness of our departure from Tucson. Repairing to a café neighboring the Alhambra, there Ah happened upon the very person of Ike Clanton.

"You, suh, are a liar and a low life scoundrel."

"Liar am I, you back shootin' murderer. I sent Wyatt after Crane so you and all them Earps might get yourselfs killt."

"Ah shot no one in the back, including your worthless father. Ah had no knowledge of any deal you made to betray your outlaw associates. Now arm yourself, and Ah shall have ma satisfaction of you."

At that, Morgan Earp appeared at ma elbow. "Easy, Doc. He ain't worth the fuss."

" 'He ain't worth the fuss,' " Ike whined. "You ain't seen no fuss yet, either of you. You will, though. More fuss than the lot of you can handle. Count on it."

On his nightly rounds, Virgil Earp entered the café drawn by the shouting. "All right, you two, break it up before I arrest the both of you."

" 'Nuther Earp come to save your sorry ass, Holliday."

"You're drunk, Ike," Virgil said. "Go sleep

184

it off now before I throw you in the hoosgow for bein' disorderly."

With that, Ike left. Wyatt, who was dining at a corner table, collected me for the walk to our respective rooms. Ike did not sleep it off as ordered. He moved to the Occidental Saloon where he continued to drink, gamble, and nurse his anger.

Hotel Glenwood
Glenwood Springs, Colorado
October 1887

Kate sat silent. The room warmed by midday sun. She cracked the window, admitting a breath of breeze.

"Tucson. I think about that October month often. We had such good times together then. No fighting. Just good times."

"They were good times."

"We had the Benson stage ruckus behind us and an outbreak of tranquility before the big dance, though we didn't know about that cotillion at the time. No, just Doc and Kate. Carefree and kickin'."

"Hasn't been a lot of carefree and kickin' left to us."

"No, there hasn't. We draw more than our share of trouble on our own. Leave us to ourselves and we do pretty good. Mix us up

185

with more like us, and it makes for a toxic brew."

"You wax philosophical."

"I'm not waxin' nothing."

"Oh, Ah think so. Quite profound, really."

"Profound my ass."

"Now don't distract me with concupiscent possibilities. Ah'm merely reflecting on your insight."

"And what insight would that be?"

"It wasn't you trouble found. It wasn't me. It wasn't even *we.* It was all of us. Likely the reason you objected to ma friendship with the Earps. Like looking in a mirror. You see them. You see us. It is the lot of us trouble has a way of finding."

"Now whose gone all phyllis-oh-sophical? I'm not looking in any mirror at them Earps."

"Are you sure?"

"Damn sure. I'm looking at a diseased dentist, the love of my life, with memories to show for it. Too many of 'em unhappy memories didn't need to be unhappy."

"They are what they are."

"They are. I'll fetch us some lunch before you unwrap this next batch of unpleasant memorabilia."

20

Ike cashed in his chips with the sunrise, moving to yet another saloon in search of still more liquid courage. He spent the morning going about town from saloon to saloon bearing his tale of woe to any who might listen. The tale he chose to tell condemned Wyatt and his brothers for the murder of his father. His grievance against me claimed Ah'd insulted his person, and he meant to have it out with me and the Earp brothers. Word of this was soon reported to Virgil by one of his officers. Wyatt, too, received reports of Ike's threats. Ah slept soundly through all of this until Kate shook me awake.

"Doc, wake up."

"Can't it keep for afternoon delight, love?"

"Not that, Doc. Mollie Fly saw Ike Clanton skulking about the vacant lot across the

187

street. He's armed."

"What time is it?"

"Nigh on eleven o'clock. What are you going to do?"

"Ah shall get dressed if Ah must, then have a bite of breakfast."

"I mean about Ike Clanton."

"Ike Clanton is a blowhard. He will take care of himself. Should he try something rash, then Ah shall deal with him."

Ah climbed out of bed. Splashed sleep out of my eyes in the wash basin on the dresser. Ah carefully selected a shirt and tie appropriate to the occasion. Mint green shirt with black silk ribbon tie in a bow.

"There's going to be trouble isn't there, Doc?"

"Bound to be where Cowboy scoundrels skulk about. I expect there will be one less son-of-a-bitch pestering the town by sunset."

"Do be careful."

Ah straightened ma tie in the looking glass above the dresser. "Careful? Ah shall take care to shoot straight and fast." Ah strapped on ma shoulder rigged Colt and shrugged into ma coat. A stylish broad brimmed black pancake hat tilted to the rakish angle Ah preferred and stood, ready to meet what might come of the day.

188

■ ■ ■ ■

Noon

Wyatt joined Virgil on his rounds. They
came upon Ike, walking down Fourth Street
armed with a rifle and pistol, in violation of
Tombstone ordinance. Virgil ordered Ike to
disarm. He refused and in a fumbling state
of inebriation attempted to go for his gun.
Virgil drew his pistol and, in a move,
reminiscent of Wyatt's Dodge City days,
struck Clanton a buffalo blow to the head,
knocking him unconscious. Disarmed, they
dragged the drunken Cowboy off to Recorder's Court where he was promptly fined for
violating the city ordinance prohibiting the
carrying of firearms. Virgil left to turn Ike's
guns over to the impound. Upon Virg taking his leave, Wyatt assured Ike if he wanted
a fight, he would meet him anytime, any-
place. Ike, for his part, continued his whin-
ing blather of grievances and threats torn
between the raging pain of his skull busting
and onset of what must have been a hang-
over of epic portion.

On leaving Recorder's Court, Wyatt next
encountered Cowboy Tom McLaury on
Fremont Street. McLaury's brash comment
concerning Wyatt's ancestry led to a scuffle

and a second buffaloing, leaving McLaury felled on the boardwalk. Tensions ran high. Nerves frayed raw. The scent of trouble fouled the air.

12:30 P.M.

All this ah would learn from Wyatt later in the day. For ma part, Ah left Fly's Boarding-house in quest of breakfast at the Alhambra. Walking south on Fourth Street, Ah observed two familiar Cowboys dismount and tie up at the Grand Hotel in the next block — Frank McLaury, Tom's older brother, and Billy Clanton, having just arrived in town. Ah sought to disarm them with charm to see if they harbored ill feelings toward me.

"Good day, Frank, Billy." Ah offered ma hand. Billy accepted it. "What brings you boys to town?"

"Business." Frank replied tersely.

"And a bit of fun," Billy added.

"Then Ah wish you good health at both business and pleasure." With that, Ah turned east on Allen Street to the Alhambra Saloon. We would later learn, Frank and Billy had yet to hear of the ruckuses involving Ike and Tom.

Leaving the Alhambra after breakfast, Ah retraced ma steps west on Allen Street where Ah found Virgil Earp standing in front of Hafford's Saloon on the corner of Allen and Fourth. Ah noted he carried a sawed-off shotgun of the sort carried by Wells Fargo shotgun messengers. The weapon suggested trouble.

"Trouble, Virg?"

He nodded. "Could be. Had to disarm Ike this morning."

"Not surprised. He was seen skulking about Fly's Boardinghouse armed. Ah suspect he was looking for me. How'd the disarming go?"

"Buffaloed him with Wyatt's help."

"Certain to improve his ill temper, Ah'll wager."

"No improvin' on that. Wyatt had a run-in with Tom McLaury 'bout an hour ago."

"And?"

"Buffaloed him, too."

"Sounds like matters are well in hand, though Ah must tell you, Frank McLaury and Billy Clanton hit town this afternoon."

"I know. Wyatt and I have been keeping an eye on the lot of 'em."

"That why you're packing the scatter gun?"

"Man can't be too careful."

He glanced over ma shoulder.

"Now what?"

Ah followed his gaze. Johnny Behan and former Sheriff Charlie Shibell hurried up the boardwalk toward us.

"What's goin down, Virgil?" Behan said by way of greeting. "Town's abuzz with talk of trouble."

"Cowboy trouble, looks like. Frank Mc-Laury and Billy Clanton just hit town to go along with Ike and Tom."

"What are you fixin' to do about it?"

"For now, nothing. They're over to the O.K. Corral. If they're fixin' to leave town, they've a right to be armed. They come our way, that's a different story."

"Then what?"

"Enforce the ordinance and disarm them. Care to help?"

"They ain't of a mind to give up their guns by the sound of all the threats they made around town. Might be best if I go have a talk with them. They see anybody spelled Earp or Holliday, for that matter, it's likely to go to gunplay."

Virgil was in a tight spot. As town marshal this was his jurisdiction. Behan had a plateful of reputational problems beneficial to Wyatt's chances of defeating him in the next election. Behan might shed some of his baggage if he could bring a dangerous situation to order without violence by trading on his cordial relations with the Cowboys. Virgil weighed all that against the best chance for taking the threat of violence down peacefully.

"Suit yourself, Johnny. Good luck."

With that, we went into Hafford's to await developments. There we found Wyatt and Morgan waiting for us.

Behan reached the O.K. Corral to find the Clantons and McLaurys gone. Looking north toward Fremont Street, he spotted a cluster of men and horses in the vacant lot across from Fly's. There he encountered the Clantons and McLaurys, now joined by gunman Billy Claiborne.

21

3 P.M.

A man unknown to me entered Hafford's.

"Is one of you gentlemen Marshal Earp?"

"I am."

"I thought I should let you know there is a group of armed men I passed on Fremont Street. I overheard threatening talk of settling matters with you and your brothers."

"Where on Fremont Street?"

"Do you know the vacant lot north of the O.K. Corral?"

"I do. Much obliged for the warning. Well, that tears it. Looks like we will have to disarm those boys. Wyatt, Morgan, you're both deputized. Come along."

As they got up to go, Ah stood. "Ah'm in on this, too. You'll recall they threatened ma life, as well." Virgil paused in thought. Ah'm sure he had his reservations. Still, Ah evened the odds."

"Give me your cane, Doc."

Ah walked with the aid of a cane due to the lingering effects of ma leg wound. "Are we going to a cotillion that makes you in need of it?"

"Masterson used one to good effect with the belligerent in Dodge."

"As Ah recall." Ah handed it over. In return, he handed me the sawed-off shotgun borrowed from Wells Fargo. Fair trade for a fight.

"Keep it under your coat. Keep an eye on the street and back us up while we do the law enforcing."

With a nod Ah concealed the coach gun as instructed. Four abreast we walked north on Fourth to Fremont. Hot wind greeted our turn west. Ah was forced to hold ma coat to cover the shotgun. Ahead, Behan could be seen in the vacant lot beside Fly's talking with the Clantons and McLaurys joined now by another. The McLaury brothers held horses adding congestion and obstructing visibility to the tight knot of men gathered in the small lot. We maintained our composure and purpose approaching the group whose new member Ah recognized as Cowboy gunman Billy Claiborne. Another gun added to the complexion of a high-risk situation.

"It would appear," Ah said. "Ike has come

lookin' for me in force."

"I say give 'em what they come for," Wyatt said.

"Should it come to that," Virgil said. "For our part, we are here to do our job."

Further up Fremont, someone shouted a warning. Behan glanced over his shoulder, said something to the Cowboys, and turned, walking briskly toward our party animated by urgency. He put up his hands.

"Gentlemen, as sheriff of this county, I must ask you to stand down. We will have no violence on my watch."

"Your coddling those boys got us into this mess," Wyatt said.

"It's the ordinance in my jurisdiction being violated here, Johnny. We will disarm those men."

"The Clantons and McLaurys are disarmed."

"I'll be the judge of that," Virgil said, leading us past Behan.

"Don't blame me if you get your-selfs killt."

Ah thought it an odd statement said in reference to men who were disarmed. Reaching the east end of the lot, Ah stationed ma-self in the middle of the street from where Ah could see the lot and be alert to the approach of any would-be interlopers come to aid their Cowboy friends. Wyatt took the end of the boardwalk in front of Fly's with Morgan in the street to his right. Virgil approached the lot.

Tom McLaury eased toward the Winchester resting in the saddle boot of the horse he held. Ah showed him the shotgun. He paused.

"Up with your hands," Virg shouted. "We've come for your weapons."

Frank McLaury reached for his gun. Wyatt drew. Billy Clanton saw Wyatt draw.

Muzzle flash bloomed bursts of powder smoke.

"Hold!" Virgil shouted to no effect.

Frank McLaury, mortally wounded, shot Virgil in the leg, knocking him down.

Seconds slowed. Pistol shots popped blaze and smoke. Ike Clanton rushed Wyatt, arms in the air, giving Billy Clanton no target. Wyatt held his fire. Morgan did not. Billy seen through smoke haze jerked by multiple bullets, still he managed to hit Morg in the shoulder. Tom McLaury made to run. Ah loosed the shotgun. He ran no more. Determined even on death's doorstep, Frank McLaury grazed ma hip with sufficient force to knock me down.

"This time I mean to finish you," he shouted.

I tossed the shotgun aside, drew my Colt, "We shall see who's finished." Ah fired as Ah rushed forward. He fell back. Ah reached him, ma *coup de gras,* a bullet to his brain.

It was over. Shooting stopped as suddenly as it started. Smoke cleared revealing the McLaury brothers dead along with Billy Clanton. Ike the coward proved himself when he fled along with Claiborne, whose reputation suffered for the indignity. Cold comfort that, in the aftermath wrought this fateful day.

Wyatt took charge of obtaining medical attention for his brothers.

Ah crossed the boardwalk to Fly's where Kate took me to our room. Ah sat on the bed, shaken. Ah shed tears for ma part in the killing. The violence escalated beyond Ike's intent to me. He provoked the confrontation and ran from it, proving himself a despicable low life coward.

"You're bleeding, Doc."

"No more than a scratch."

"Let's have a look at that. Drop your pants."

Ah did, numbed by events of the last quarter hour. Kate busied herself with water basin and towel cleansing the wound and binding it with improvised bandaging to staunch the bleeding. Ah was left to wonder what might become of all this.

We had not long to wait.

Friday, October 28, 1881

Cochise county Coroner Henry Mathews called a coroner's inquest into the deaths of Billy Clanton and the McLaury brothers two days later to which Ah and the Earps were required to appear. Ten jurors were selected by the coroner to hear testimony of such witnesses as the coroner felt pertinent to the matter. Under Arizona territorial law, the jury was empaneled to determine if charges were warranted. We, of course, fully expected to be exonerated, that is until Johnny Behan took the stand.

"The Cochise County Coroner's inquest into the events of a gunfight in the vicinity of the O.K. Corral on October twenty-sixth, 1881, is now in session. Let the record show Henry Mathews, coroner presiding. I call Sheriff Behan as first witness. Please take the stand."

Behan did so with feigned sobriety and a glint in his eye.

"Do you solemnly swear to tell the truth, the whole truth, and nothing but the truth?"

"I do."

"Be seated. Now, Sheriff Behan, were you witness to the gunfight giving rise to this inquest?"

"I was."

"Then tell the jury what you observed."

"On the morning of the twenty-sixth, I received word there might be trouble between the Clantons, McLaurys, and Earps. I found Marshal Earp at Hafford's Saloon, keeping an eye on the situation. The marshal told me Ike and Billy Clanton along with Frank and Tom McLaury were at the O.K. Corral armed. On the pretense of leaving town, carrying weapons posed no problem. Should they leave the corral armed, Marshal Earp meant to enforce city ordinance and disarm them. Given the appearance of hostility between the parties, I offered my assistance to disarm any who might come into violation of the ordinance against the carrying of firearms in town. We agreed. . . ."

"We agreed?"

"Marshal Earp and I agreed I should approach the Clantons and McLaurys to make sure they did not leave the corral armed unless they were leaving town. I walked over to the corral only to find the boys had left and could now be seen in the vacant lot next to Fly's Boardinghouse."

"What action did you take then?"

"I approached Ike and Frank and asked them to turn over their guns to me."

"They were armed then?"

"Some were, some were not. I couldn't be sure who was and who was not."

"And did those who were armed turn over their weapons?"

"We were discussing it when someone shouted a warning. When I looked east on Fremont Street, I saw Marshal Earp approaching with his brothers, Wyatt and Morgan, along with Doc Holliday."

"What did you do?"

"I went to meet them to head off the risk of a confrontation. As I approached, one of them ordered me out of the way saying the Clantons were spoiling for a fight, and they were going to get it. I assured the marshal the boys had no intention to fight as they passed me by. At that point I followed. Next thing I knew guns were drawn and fired, the first being a nickel-plated revolver."

Ah must admit Ah reacted to the suggestion Ah started the fight as Ah was well known to carry such a firearm. Behan's account of the events of the shoot-out came with colorful embellishments calculated to cast doubt on our having acted in self-defense. His assertion someone in our party called out reference to Ike's threatening demands for a fight we intended to make good on never happened. His statement that

201

the deceased declared they were unarmed with no intent to fight was not born out by the facts. According to Behan we drew our weapons and fired, with the first shot coming from, "A nickel plated pistol." He did not mention me by name, but his lie was clearly intended to implicate me in starting the fight. In so claiming, Behan sought to charge me with responsibility for the whole ugly affair. It was to be only the beginning of false accusations made upon ma person by those who thought Ah might be easier to incriminate than the chief of police and duly sworn deputies.

Mathews next called Billy Claiborne, who not surprisingly, recollected events much as Behan testified. He next called Ike Clanton, whose account of the fight agreed with Behan, though his testimony began with our encounter in the Alhambra Café the night before. After Behan's fanciful rendition of events leading to the start of the fight, Ah could barely contain ma anticipation for the testimony of a bloated popinjay the likes of Ike Clanton. Ah was not to be disappointed.

"Do you solemnly swear to tell the truth, the whole truth, and nothing but the truth?"

"I do."

"Mister Clanton, this inquiry has heard testimony suggesting certain events on the evening of October twenty-fifth contributed to hostilities toward the Earp brothers."

"Sure did."

"Please tell the jury what happened."

"Doc Holliday called me out and threatened me, he did. I went to the Alhambra Café for a bite to eat when he come after me. Told me if I was looking for a fight, he'd be more than pleased to accommodate me. I told him I was unarmed. He told me to arm myself."

"And did you?"

"No, sir. 'Bout that time Marshal Earp come along to take Holliday's side. I thought better of it all and left."

"And that settled it?"

"No, sir. Next morning, I armed myself in defense against Holliday's threats. That's when I run into Marshal Earp and his brother Wyatt. They pistol whipped me for ma gun and run me into Recorder's Court. Pistol whipped Tom McLaury that morning, too, though poor Tom ain't here to tell his tale."

Hotel Glenwood
Glenwood Springs, Colorado
October 1887
Kate returned with soup, soft-boiled eggs, and toast.

"This is lunch? Here Ah thought Ah was dying of consumption." *Cugh, cugh . . . cugh, cugh.* "Turns out it's starvation."

"You'll not starve as long as I take care of you. Now eat. You need your strength."

Ah took a spoon of egg with a bite of toast.

Kate sat shaking her head.

"What are you thinking?"

"Back to the fight."

"What of it?"

"If it weren't for the Earps, not your fight. But for them, it was not only your fight, but your fault."

"Wasn't ma fault. That was politics."

"Weren't your politics, either."

She had a point, much as Ah hated to admit it. So, Ah didn't.

22

Saturday, October 29, 1881

From these proceedings it became clear, Behan saw the gunfight for an opportunity to rid himself of Wyatt opposing him in the next election. The Cowboy faction rallied around the lies hoping to rid themselves of the Earps and anyone who supported them, ma-self included. The fact we were given no opportunity to speak in our own defense, suggested the coroner himself may have had a desire to see us tried. The jury reached their verdict the following day. Ah suspect opinion divided among them. Their verdict simply stated in effect, the deceased died by our hands.

Ike Clanton filed complaints in Justice Wells Spicer's court alleging the deceased were murdered. Justice Spicer issued warrants accordingly and Behan arrested Wyatt and me, sparing Morg and Virg incarceration out of consideration for their wounds.

Justice Spicer set our bail at ten thousand dollars each. A handsome sum we were able to raise with the help of Wyatt's well-to-do friends.

Justice Spicer next held a hearing on the matter. The hearing before Justice Spicer was preliminary to determining the need to convene a grand jury. Ah was represented by attorney T. J. Drum. Wyatt and his brothers employed defense lawyer Tom Fitch, who by agreement led the defense. Prosecution fell to county attorney Lyttleton Price, a man not known to be sympathetic to Cowboy interests. Ike Clanton's lawyer, Ben Goodrich, persuaded Price to allow him to join the prosecution. Price agreed, a concession destined to prove troublesome as events would proceed.

In preparing our defense, attorney Fitch advised our best chance of acquittal was before Justice Spicer. Prospects for a grand jury sympathetic to the Cowboy faction in Cochise County were simply too great to risk if the risk could be avoided. Given testimonies at the coroner's inquest, it became clear the Cowboy faction, to which Behan was most certainly allied, meant to make me accountable for starting the fight. Fitch advised we build our defense on officers of the law doing their duty. That risked revealing a defense we might use should the proceedings go to trial, though Fitch reckoned the gamble worth taking to obtain a verdict before Justice Spicer and avoid a higher risk proceeding at trial. For ma part, Ah was to sit quietly by, secure in the fact Ah did not fire the first shot. "Sitting quietly by" ran contrary to ma nature, but under the circumstances Ah was strongly advised to curb ma-self. Ah then became an observer at ma own "preliminary hearing."

Monday, October 31, 1881
The morning dawned cool and clear with the feel of autumn in the air. Wyatt and Ah were in attendance, Virgil and Morgan having been once again excused owing to their wounds. The hearing convened in the Cochise County Courthouse on Fremont within eyesight of the vacant lot, scene of the fight with a distinguished, black-robed Justice Spicer presiding.

The prosecution opened with the coroner testifying as to the verdict of the coroner's inquest. The inquest verdict assigned little by way of blame merely stating the obvious. Ike Clanton's charge of first-degree murder, on the other hand, presented a difficult standard in a case where officers of the law were engaged in performance of their duties. The defense knew this as did the prosecution. As expected, the prosecution directed its case against me, resorting to Behan's testimony of a nickel-plated revolver having begun the shooting. By reputation, Ah became the easier case to send to trial. The curb on ma nature was to be sorely tested over the coming weeks. Ah spoke of it with attorney Fitch.

"Must Ah sit here and be tried by Behan's lies?"

"Be patient, Doc. I know it is difficult, but truth is on our side, and we will bring it before Justice Spicer in due course. It is to our advantage to let the prosecution take its best shots such that we have sound rebuttal on which to make our case."

"Ah do hope you are right in your assessment, as it is ma neck as might be stretched should our rebuttal fall short."

"I understand the . . . concern. Please understand we are in the earliest stages of the proceedings. Much more will be said on both sides. Likely it will grow darker before the dawn. Trust the truth. Lady justice balances her scale."

Ah appreciated Tom's confidence. It did little to loosen the collar of consequences awaiting me.

■ ■ ■ ■

Tuesday, November 1

Court convened a second idyllic morning to the prosecution continuing their case. Witnesses portrayed the Cowboys as innocent men, preparing to leave town. Some among them who were not armed attempted to comply with the police order to put up their hands when Ah pulled ma pistol and opened fire, causing Cowboys who were armed to defend themselves. The Earps then returned fire killing Billy Clanton and the McLaury brothers. Ah bit ma tongue on the repeated lie, though Ah admit Ah might have shaken ma head if only to appease ma own righteous anger.

In cross examining Behan and another of the witnesses testifying to ma having fired the first shot, attorney Fitch established the fact Ah carried a shotgun to the gunfight, a weapon requiring the use of both hands, thereby casting doubt on testimony claiming Ah drew ma pistol and fired first. While this was helpful to ma case, the prosecution established the shotgun had also been discharged while reasserting the Cowboys were attempting to comply with Virgil's order when the shooting started, killing three of them. Pistol or shotgun, the implication remained Ah had started the shootout. All things considered, prospects for the defense did not appear favorable.

Tom Fitch raised objection to a leading line of questioning Ben Goodrich, Ike's attorney, pursued with one of the prosecution witnesses to the shooting. Justice Spicer overruled Tom's objection. Fitch then reminded Justice Spicer that as a Justice of the Peace he was to record testimony rather than rule as to admissibility. Justice Spicer assured counsel he would rule liberally as to admissibility. An accommodation we should later put to good use.

Thursday, November 4
Will McLaury, brother to Frank and Tom, arrived in Tombstone from Texas on November 3. A lawyer, Will was bent on avenging his brothers' deaths. He made clear he meant to see their killers tried for murder and hanged. By noon recess on the first day, having observed the prosecution being conducted by Lyttleton Price and Ben Goodrich, McLaury had seen enough. He asked Justice Spicer if he might join the prosecution. Spicer agreed, with Lyttleton Price allowing him to take over the case. The scoundrel was quick to grasp ma vulner-

ability to the outcome he wished to pursue, likely at the behest of Ike Clanton.

Having heard witnesses testify as to the altercations leading to the gunfight, Tom McLaury raising his hands unarmed, and the shooting begun by ma-self and Morgan Earp, Will McLaury requested Justice Spicer have Wyatt and me reincarcerated, as was the practice in capital murder cases. Spicer agreed raising our bond to twenty-one thousand dollars each. And thus, Wyatt and Ah were taken into custody in the Cochise County Jail.

Ah must say that weekend in jail may have been the longest two days of ma life. Wyatt, who could be taciturn in the best of times, was sour and sullen at the events of the trial. Will McLaury knew his business and was clearly having his way with Justice Spicer and our defense. Ah asked Behan for a deck of cards. Ah thought a few friendly hands might cheer Wyatt. He would have none of it. It left me to brood in bad humor and boredom. Had Johnny Behan made good his penchant for jail breaks, Ah believe Ah should have made a run for it. Not that such action would have gotten me very far. Cowboy escapees could lose themselves in rough country. By ma own admission such circumstances ill-suited me.

■ ■ ■ ■

Monday, November 8

Clouds rolled A thick blanket of grey felt over Tombstone that day suited to the proceedings unfolding inside the court-house. Billy Claiborne took the stand. His version of the events of the gunfight agreed with ma having fired first even though the Cowboys had raised their hands. He then added a grisly account of Morgan, standing close enough to Billy Clanton to put his pistol to Billy's head and firing point blank. He described Billy's powder-burn blackened face and shattered skull as a nightmare the like of which he had never seen before. At that, our situation could not have been seen for worse. Will McLaury sensed the moment of victory and sought to follow up Claiborne's gruesome account with a last damning witness. He called Ike Clanton.

Tuesday, November 9

We trooped into court that day, Wyatt and Ah, with a palpable sense of foreboding hanging over us. To this point it would have been hard to imagine our situation having gotten any worse. Ike testified to the events leading to the gunfight in harmony with the testimonies of previous prosecution witnesses. He and his brother and the McLaury brothers were cooperating with Sheriff Behan's request to disarm or leave town when the Earps and that man, he pointed an accusatory finger at me, came to do their murderous deeds. Tom Fitch objected to the witness reaching such a conclusion. Justice Spicer overruled the objection, letting Ike's accusation stand.

Given the length of Ike's stay on the witness stand, Justice Spicer adjourned the court to reconvene at 10:00 a.m. Thursday for cross examination by the defense. Much as Ah hated the prospect of two more days in jail, the recess gave defense counsel a breather to be put to good use.

Tom Fitch spent a good part of the recess going over the events of October 26 with Wyatt. He wanted to understand the details of Wyatt's agreement with Ike to hand over the Benson stage robbers and Ike's fear that Wyatt had spoken of the deal with me. Ike knew if the Cowboys found out he betrayed them, he'd be a dead man. Ma confrontation with Ike in the Alhambra café, late of the evening of October 25, was meant to assure Ike Wyatt had not betrayed his confidence. Ah listened to the jailhouse conversations with no notion of how any of that might benefit our cause. Will McLaury, it seemed, had us headed for a grand jury trial and likely trip to the gallows.

Thursday, November 11

Justice spicer called the proceeding to order, reseating Ike and reminding him he was still under oath.

"Mister McLaury, I believe you still have the witness. Are there any further questions?"

"Nothing further at this time, Your Honor."

"Very well, then. Mister Fitch, your witness."

Fitch rose, clasped his hands behind his back, and approached the witness stand. Morning sun, shining brightly through the courthouse windows at his back, shadowed Ike's face until Fitch stepped aside.

"Now, Mister Clanton, on the evening of October twenty-fifth when you encountered John Henry Holliday in the Alhambra Saloon Café, had you been drinking?"

"I'd had a couple of drinks."

"A couple of drinks. Could you clarify that for us? Would that be more than two or fewer than ten?"

"I don't know. I drink 'em. I don't count 'em."

"Approximately what time did you encounter Doctor Holliday?"

"Little after midnight, I reckon."

"And what time did you arrive at the Alhambra?"

Ike shrugged, "Eight o'clock or so."

"Four hours before you encountered Doctor Holliday. Were you drunk when you confronted Doctor Holliday?"

"He confronted me."

"All right then, were you drunk when he confronted you?"

"Objection, Your Honor. Counsel is badgering the witness."

"Your Honor, Mister Clanton's sobriety leading up to these events is material to his testimony."

"Overruled, Mister McLaury. You may proceed, Mister Fitch."

"Thank you, Your Honor. Mister Clanton, at a little after midnight on the evening of October twenty-fifth, were you drunk?"

"I may have been some."

Under continued cross examination Ike admitted to continuing his drinking the morning of the twenty-sixth while going about town armed and telling anyone who would listen, he meant to kill ma-self and the Earps on sight. Fitch then turned his line of questioning in a direction certain to shake Ike's composure. Ah remember this moment vividly.

"I hold here in my hand a telegram sent from Wells Fargo to their Tombstone agent Marshall Williams, it reads, 'Reward offered for Benson stage robbers is dead or alive.' " He showed the telegram to Ike. "Have you ever seen this before?"

Ike hemmed and hawed.

"Have you ever seen this before?"

Ike looked around the court room like a cornered rat. He nodded.

"Let the record show the witness admits to having seen the telegram in question. And who showed this telegram to you, Mister Clanton?"

"Wyatt Earp."

"Why did Wyatt Earp show you the telegram?"

"He wanted me to help him track down Leonard, Head, and Crane."

"Did he offer you the reward for your help?"

"Objection, Your Honor. The witness is not on trial here. Counselor's questioning is irrelevant."

"Your Honor, Ike Clanton's behaviors and motives for those behaviors leading up to the events in question are material to those events and actions taken by defendants in this proceeding."

"Objection overruled. You may proceed, Mister Fitch."

"Thank you, Your Honor. Now, Mister Clanton, did Wyatt Earp offer you the reward money if you assisted him in finding the men implicated in the attempted Benson stage holdup and murders?"

"He did."

"Did you agree to help him?"

"I thought about it and turned him down. Didn't matter, as it turned out we never got the chance to do nothin' cause they was all killt before we could."

"Did Wyatt Earp tell you why he wanted to track these men down?"

At that, Ike looked as though he'd been let out of the corner. Like a rat he went for the cheese.

"Wyatt wanted 'em killt, cause he and Morgan give the Wells Fargo cash to Doc Holliday and Billy Leonard before the stage left Tombstone. He figured Leonard, Head, and Crane for the only three who could call him out for his part in the robbery."

"That is a most startling admission, Mister Clanton. How is it you never notified Sheriff Behan?"

"I give my word I wouldn't."

Tom had no further questions. Will Mc-

217

Laury, not knowing how much damage Ike's testimony had done the prosecution's case, asked Justice Spicer for a redirect examination of the witness. Permission was granted.

"Mister Clanton, were you surprised by Wyatt Earp's admission of his role in the Benson stage robbery?"

"Not really. A few days after the robbery, I overheard Doc Holliday braggin' to Virgil Earp how he'd killt Bud Philpot during the holdup attempt."

"Virgil Earp is chief of police, is he not? What did he have to say about that?"

"Said he led the posse to let Leonard, Head, and Crane get way."

"The crimes you describe, robbery and murder, are serious crimes. Why have you waited until now to come forward?"

"Like I said, I give my word. That, and I was afraid for my life seein' what happened to Leonard, Head, and Crane. After the gunfight and them killin' Billy, Frank, and Tom, I knew something had to be done. When you called me to this here stand and swore me under oath, it was time."

"No further questions. The prosecution rests."

Court adjourned.

23

Friday, November 12

Ah'm sure will and Ike thought they had the lot of us right where they wanted us, headed for the gallows by way of a grand jury trial. And all of it owing to Ike's wild lies. That house of cards could be easily brought down by the mere fact that the Benson stage Wells Fargo shipment had been safely delivered. That no theft occurred would come as a shock to McLaury. Foolish Ike should have known such a lie could not hold water for long. Tom Fitch was not about to let it go at that. He and Wyatt put their heads together again. When court convened the following morning, Fitch opened the defense with a startling announcement.

"Your Honor, the defense wishes to exercise its prerogative under Arizona Territorial law to open its case with the narrative statement of Wyatt Earp."

"Clarification, Your Honor. The defense is calling Wyatt Earp as a witness, is it not?"

"In preliminary hearings under Arizona law, Mister McLaury, testimony is permitted to be entered into the record by narrative statement without the formalities of examination and cross examination. It is a provision of territorial law that allows the court to get to the meat of a matter efficiently."

"Your Honor, I must object in the strongest possible terms. I have never heard of anything as irregular as this."

"Heard of it or not, Mister McLaury, it's the law in Arizona."

"But, Your Honor!"

"Mister McLaury, I advise you to take a seat before this court finds you in contempt."

"No need to go looking for contempt." McLaury slumped into his seat at the prosecution table, wearing contempt as plainly as the cravat at his throat.

"You may proceed, Mister Fitch."

Tom's clever use of a little-known provision in territorial law caught McLaury completely by surprise. Justice Spicer, having earlier agreed to be open with respect to admissibility, allowed Wyatt to take the stand with a prepared written statement.

Wyatt delivered a convincing commanding performance, the meat of which began
with the Benson stage robbery establishing
safe delivery of the Wells Fargo shipment.
At which McLaury clasped his temples as
though in physical pain. Ah could only
hope.

Wyatt went on to describe tracking the
robbers to the Redfield ranch and the
capture of Luther King who identified
Leonard, Head, and Crane as those responsible for shooting Bud Philpot and the passenger. King, having been taken into custody by Sheriff Behan, promptly escaped
jail. Ah know Wyatt couldn't resist rubbing
Johnny's nose in that old horse dropping.

He continued to explain his intent to run
for Cochise County Sheriff and thought to
advance his cause by capturing Leonard,
Head, and Crane where his prospective opponent could not. More Behan horse drop-
pings. He described asking Ike Clanton and
Frank McLaury to assist in helping to draw
the fugitives into a trap. Ike was willing to
consider doing so for the reward money,
though he feared they would not be taken
without a fight and wanted assurance the
Wells Fargo reward offer would be paid
dead or alive. Marshall Williams contacted
Wells Fargo with the question and received

the telegram earlier entered in evidence by way of a response.

Later, Ike and Frank McLaury claimed Wyatt had revealed their deal to Marshall Williams and ma-self. We knew this for frequent reported threats to our lives. Wyatt explained ma purpose in approaching Ike at the Alhambra the evening of the twenty-fifth was to assure him Wyatt had revealed nothing of any dealings between the two of them to me. He went on to speak of Ike's drunken ravings while illegally armed on the streets the morning of October 26. How he assisted Virgil in subduing and disarming Ike to have him appear before the Recorder's Court as provided by city ordinance. The scuffle with Tom McLaury resulted from McLaury's threats of a fight.

He confirmed conversations between Behan and Virgil while deciding what to do about disarming the Clantons and McLaurys at the OK Corral and receiving word the Cowboys had left the corral in violation of Tombstone city ordinance. He stated Virgil deputized himself and Morgan to assist in enforcing the ban on carrying firearms and Virgil's request of me to cover their backs. He made clear Behan's claim the boys were disarmed as we passed along Fremont to the vacant lot.

The gunfight broke out when Billy Clanton went for his gun. Wyatt testified he and Billy exchange the first shots. If Tom McLaury were unarmed, we did not know it, as Sheriff Behan's earlier claim of having disarmed the Cowboys had clearly proven to be false. Wyatt closed his account of the fight saying we approached the encounter with the intent to enforce city ordinance in the performance of official duties. The fight became a matter of self-defense. This last came with a short campaign speech concerning his law enforcement experience and having faced similar situations in the past.

Fitch next called witnesses to Ike's belligerent drunken behavior about town on the morning of the twenty-sixth. McLaury's cross examinations dismissed all this as being irrelevant to the events of the fight at which Ike was unarmed. As to Ike's credibility as a witness, there was little McLaury could do to repair the damage already done. Still, something more was needed.

Fitch decided to call Virgil Earp.

Cosmopolitan Hotel
Saturday, November 19
Justice Spicer called a special session to order in a private dining room in the hotel where Virgil and Morgan were recovering

from their wounds. Virgil chose to testify rather than enter a statement into the record and was sworn in by Justice Spicer. Under Fitch's questioning, Virgil recounted his part in events of the evening of the twenty-fifth, as occurred at the Alhambra Café. He testified on waking the morning of the twenty-sixth to learn Ike was about town armed, threatening a fight to finish the Earps. He described disarming Ike and taking him before the Recorder's Court. Fitch picked up questioning leading to the gunfight.

"Upon learning Ike, his brother, and the McLaurys were at the O.K. Corral, what did you do?"

"As long as they were at the corral, they posed no threat to the citizenry and could safely be seen as leaving town. When Sheriff Behan came by, I asked him to help me disarm them."

"And what was Sheriff Behan's response?"

"He said he would disarm them alone as they would not surrender their weapons to me."

"And did he disarm them?"

"He went down to the O.K. Corral. A short time later, a man previously unknown to me, informed us the Cowboys were on Fremont Street threatening to kill the Earps and Doc Holliday. If they were still armed, this placed them in violation of the city ordinance prohibiting the carrying of firearms while representing a danger to the community. I determined the need to investigate and if necessary, disarm them. I was accompanied at the time by deputies Wyatt and Morgan Earp who I asked to assist me."

"And John H. Holliday?"

"I asked Doc to accompany us to keep watch on the street as I knew there were those sympathetic to the Cowboys who might be about."

"So, in your judgement as chief of police, you had a dangerous situation that needed to be addressed in the interest of public safety. Is that correct?"

"It is."

"What happened next?"

"We reached Fremont Street and turned west toward the vacant lot beside Fly's Boardinghouse where the Cowboys were gathered with Sheriff Behan. Johnny saw us coming and came down the street to meet us."

"What did Sheriff Behan have to say?"

"He said they were disarmed. We soon learned this was not the case."

"Your Honor, if I might beg the court's indulgence, I can see Mister Earp is tiring.

Might we adjourn this proceeding and continue at a later time?"

Spicer glanced at Will McLaury. "Counselor?"

"No objection."

"Then this court stands adjourned."

Ah must say whilst rotting in the Cochise County Jail, this "preliminary hearing" might rival a session of the territorial legislative in length. At least the gloom hanging over the proceedings had lightened some, Ike's testimony and Wyatt's statement having thrown the prosecution back on its heels. It was far too soon to feel celebratory for the matter would ultimately rest in Justice Spicer's hands. Yet there seemed a glimmer of hope lady fortune might find her way to smile upon us.

24

Cosmopolitan Hotel
Tuesday, November 22

Justice Spicer reconvened court, reminding Virgil he was still under oath. Again, under questioning by Tom Fitch, Virgil's account of the gunfight followed closely Wyatt's earlier statement, leaving little for Will McLaury to cross examine. He did pick at a curious detail.

"Mister Earp, you testified you were alerted to the presence of the Clanton McLaury party on Fremont Street by a man previously unknown to you. Do you know who that man is?"

"I believe his name is Sills."

"And he was previously unknown to you prior to October the twenty-sixth when he warned you?"

"That is correct."

"Curious you wouldn't know him in your capacity as chief of police. Tombstone is not that big."

Virg shrugged. "Maybe he's new in town."

"Do you know where Mister Sills is from?"

"I do not."

"Did anyone else hear Mister Sills warning of the Clanton McLaury party's intentions?"

"I was alone in front of Hafford's Saloon at the time."

"Have you seen or spoken to Mister Sills since these events?"

"Matter of fact, I saw him just yesterday, though I did not speak to him."

"You saw him yesterday? Where did you see Mister Sills?"

"Passed through the lobby of this hotel."

"No further questions, Your Honor."

Justice Spicer then adjourned the hearing to resume at the courthouse following recess for lunch.

Cochise County Courthouse
Tuesday Afternoon

"All rise," the bailiff intoned.

Justice Spicer took his seat. "Mister Fitch, you may proceed."

"Thank you, Your Honor. The defense calls H. F. Sills."

Will McLaury buried his face in his hands. Ah must say Ah took delight in his

228

gesture of despair. Ah was as surprised as anyone by the appearance of the mysterious Mister Sills called to the witness stand.

A shortish man, squarish of feature with a bushy beard flecked in grey came forward from the back of the courtroom to the witness stand. He glanced around the courtroom blinking.

"Raise your right hand. Do you solemnly swear to tell the truth, the whole truth, and nothing but the truth, so help you God?"

"I do."

"Be seated."

"Now, Mister Sills, do you reside in Tombstone?"

"No, sir, my home is Las Vegas, New Mexico."

"Then what brings you to Tombstone?"

"I'm an engineer for the Atchison, Topeka & Santa Fe railroad on lay over."

"On October twenty-sixth, did you take it upon yourself to warn police chief Virgil Earp of a dangerous situation he needed to be aware of?"

"I did."

"And how did you come to this decision?"

"Walking down Fremont Street I overheard a group of men talking loudly about killing the Earps and Doc Holliday on sight."

"Did you know who they were talking about?"

"I may have heard the names, but I didn't know who they were. I thought it important enough to inquire as to who these men were speaking of and where they might be found."

"And so, you were directed to Chief Earp."

"I was."

"After warning the chief, what did you do?"

"I followed the chief and his deputies up Fremont Street to the lot where the gang was waiting."

"Objection, Your Honor. Five citizens in a vacant lot do not constitute a gang."

"Sustained. Please confine your testimony to the facts as you observed them, Mister Sills."

"Sorry, Your Honor."

"Mister Sills," Fitch continued. "Tell this court what you observed from your vantage point on Fremont Street."

"I heard someone order the men to raise their hands. Two drew their pistols."

"Stop right there for a moment, Mister Sills." With that Fitch came to ma place at the defense table. "Were either of those pistols nickel plated?"

230

"No, sir."

"Are you sure?"

"Nickle plated in broad daylight. I surely would have noticed."

"Now look closely at this gentleman. Was this man either of the two who drew their pistols?"

"No, sir. I believe that man was armed with a sawed-off shotgun."

"Thank you, Mister Sills. You may continue."

Sills's account of the gunfight squared with the accounts given by Wyatt and Virgil. On cross examination McLaury sought to find something to discredit Sills or impugn the integrity of his character. In this he failed.

Fitch then called a series of witnesses to Ike's behavior and threats the morning of the twenty-sixth, these now having greater weight with respect to Clanton McLaury's intentions to kill us. Facing lethal force in the enforcement of the law, we were justified in responding as we did. Ah must say, jail or no, Ah slept better that night than Ah had in some while.

With our case having advanced beyond allegations and false testimony, Fitch asked Justice Spicer to release Wyatt and me on bail. This he did fixing bond at twenty

231

thousand dollars each. Wyatt's many friends were able to raise his. Ah was only released when Wyatt encouraged those who supported him to join him in doing the right thing by me.

Cochise County Courthouse
Tuesday, November 29

Fitch began winding up our case calling two witnesses who testified to seeing Tom Mc-Laury carry a concealed pistol dispelling the assertion he was unarmed. A witness to Johnny Behan's bedside visit with Virgil the night of the fight, heard him discuss the events of the day with Virgil in a manor drastically different from his sworn testimony before Justice Spicer and in details consistent with the testimonies of Wyatt, Virgil, and Mr. Sills.

Justice Spicer adjourned the proceedings to come to his decision.

Cochise County Courthouse
Wednesday, November 30

Justice Spicer reached his decision the following day. In his opinion he affirmed actions taken on our part were consistent with sworn duty to enforce the law. He was critical of Virgil's choices to assist him, a criticism Ah suspect he directed at me, though he said as events played out, Virgil needed the support of his deputies. He noted discrepancies in the various witnesses' accounts of the events of October 26, and as such he relied on the testimony of H.F. Sills and its agreement with the statement given by Wyatt Earp and the testimony of Virgil Earp. He stated the Cochise County Grand Jury could certainly choose to consider the case, but he saw no cause to refer the matter for trial. In December, the grand jury concurred with Justice Spicer's opinion, and the matter at law came to an end.

Hotel Glenwood
Glenwood Springs, Colorado
October 1887
Kate cleared away the supper tray and trimmed the lamp to restful dim light and shadow.

"Join me for a drink?" *Cugh, cugh . . . cugh.*

"Drink don't sound like such a good idea."

"You'd deny a dying man his comforts? At this point, darlin', what difference does it make?"

"I suppose not. After listening to all that, I could use one myself."

She poured and handed me a glass.

Poured one for herself and took her seat beside the bed, fortified with a belt.

"Had yourself some pretty fair lawyerin' there, didn't you?"

"Tom Fitch? Likely saved us a jury trial and me the gallows, though Ah'm not sure that wouldn't have been quicker, all things considered." Ah consoled ma-self with a swallow.

"Now, Doc, you don't really mean that."

Ah lifted a brow.

"The hangin' part, I mean."

"No. Ah suppose not. There was plenty more to come for sure."

"Yes, there was. Like life — some of it good and some of it not so good."

Ah closed ma eyes and let ma thoughts drift on to events yet to come.

"Hold your thoughts for now. You need some rest. Plenty of time to get on with it in the morning."

She took the empty glass from ma fingers. Brushed a kiss on ma forehead. Picked up the glasses and supper tray. Huffed out the lamp to darkness and left by the soft click of the door latch.

Ah woke. Cold sweat. My heart raced. A dream. Ah remembered. Hoofbeats coming hard and fast. Ma chest heaved. Ah slowed ma breathing wet with expectorant. Grey light. Another dawn. Another day. How many . . . more? Ah lie there staring into shadows. Nothing for me to do but wait. Wait for? This day, wait for Kate. Grey light turned gold. The door latch clicked. Ah opened ma eyes.

"Mornin', Doc."

"Ah believe it is. Another morning. Coffee smells good."

"Bacon and eggs to go with it."

"Ah believe Ah shall turn into an egg."

"Heavenly days, not as bad as all that."

"Heaven has little to do with it, darlin'."

"You could speak of it with Father Downey when he next comes to visit."

"Ah welcome his friendship and kindly concern for ma wellbeing. A life-long Methodist sinner is likely beyond his calling."

"You'll never know unless you ask."

"Ah shall consider it."

"Good, now eat your eggs. They're good for you."

"You do see to ma comforts."

25

Justice may have been served at law, but the court of public opinion remained very much in session. Law-abiding citizens and the business community were satisfied Justice Spicer had considered the evidence and come to a fair and reasonable verdict. Such was not the case with Will McLaury, Ike Clanton, their Cowboy confederates, and the small ranchers who made common cause with them. They felt themselves denied justice by a court representative of a government they disliked and distrusted. If justice were to be done, it would be up to them to do it. Almost from the moment the gavel rang down on the verdict, word about town had us all for marked men.

Veins of blood feud run deep. Virgil, Wyatt, Morgan, and Ah were rumored murder targets. Others also said to be on some death list included Justice Spicer, Tom Fitch, and Wells Fargo agent Marshall Williams. Some said the list even included Mayor John Clum. The conjecture seemed far-fetched until events gave credence to rumor, credence attendant to attempted murder.

That December, Mayor Clum, having decided not to seek a second term, departed Tombstone for an extended trip to Washington, D.C. Before the stage he was on reached Benson, it was attacked by masked gunmen. Racing through the night along perilous roadway, the driver managed to guide the bullet-riddled coach to the safety of a waystation. A terrified Clum, convinced the attackers meant to assassinate him, obtained use of a horse and rode through the night to reach the railhead in Benson.

Soon after word of the attack reached Tombstone, Ah was in the Alhambra with Wyatt and Virgil. Milt Joyce saw us there and confronted Virgil. Ah suspect he had no stomach for Wyatt or me.

"Did you hear, Virgil, the Benson stage was attacked?"

"I heard. Thankfully no one was hurt."

"I'm sure you're thankful. For myself, I've been expecting it since your brothers and Holliday there got let out of jail."

Ah started to leave ma chair. Wyatt barred ma way with his arm and a glance that said

"Let Virg handle it." Ah sat back down, though ma temper bristled. Ah'd had about as much of Milt Joyce as ma good humor could stand.

"Milt, you got no call, makin' wild accusations like that."

"Hell, everyone knows they was wound up in the last murderous holdup attempt."

Virg slapped him across the face so hard the man staggered.

Joyce backed away. "You back-shootin' son-of-a-bitch! I ain't healed. Next time I will be — face to face."

That ended things for the moment. The next evening Joyce returned to the Alhambra healed. This time he challenged Wyatt and me.

"You boys ready to finish what you started last night?"

"If Ah must, you pissant nuisance."

"He ain't worth the trouble, Doc," Wyatt said.

Whereupon, Johnny Behan stepped in.

"Give me the gun, Milt. I'm going to save your life and take you to Recorder's Court for carrying a firearm illegally."

The Benson stage shooting was followed by a threatening letter to Justice Spicer advising him to leave town. He refused and did so both publicly and defiantly. With threats of violence growing in intensity, Wyatt suggested we all move to the Cosmopolitan Hotel where we might find safety in numbers. The Cosmopolitan offered a view across Allen Street to the Grand Hotel where the Cowboys would stay when in town. Ah declined, preferring ma comforts at Fly's. Kate did not share ma comfort.

"We can't stay here, Doc. Even the Earps are moving to the Cosmopolitan for safety. Come to Globe with me."

"Ah'll not run out on ma friends, much less be intimidated by a rabble of rustlers."

"You stay with the Earps, you're gonna get yourself killed."

"Ah am walking dead as we speak, darlin'. It makes little difference if Ah walk with ma friends or walk alone, Ah'll be walking just the same."

"Makes a difference to me. I'm leavin' for Globe."

December 28, 1881
Ma disregard of Cowboy capacity for treachery and depredation did not last long. Even in the goodwill spirit of the holiday season, peace could not abide in the hearts of evil violent men. Late of an evening at cards, Virgil left the Oriental Saloon for the short walk to the Cosmopolitan. As he made

to cross Fifth Street on Allen, assassins cut loose with shotguns from ambush. At the sound of gunfire, Wyatt ran from the Oriental to his aid. He found his brother severely wounded yet attempting to reach the Cosmopolitan. This they were able to accomplish, and with prompt medical attention, Virg survived his wounds. He forbade amputation of his badly damaged left arm, which afforded him no further use for the rest of his life.

Wyatt had seen enough. Bystanders observed two, possibly three, men fleeing the scene, though no positive identifications could be made owing to darkness. This left identification of suspects to speculation. While several Cowboys were known to be capable of such villainy, strong suspicion fell on Ike Clanton along with Frank Stilwell having played a part. With Behan the only law in the county, Wyatt determined any action taken would be up to him, legally if possible, but taken, nonetheless. Virgil, suspended as city marshal over the gunfight, had not been reinstated following our exoneration. He still held a Deputy U.S. Marshal position, the duties for which he could no longer perform. Wyatt contacted U.S. Marshal for Arizona Territory Crawley Dake in Prescott, describing the situation and requesting he be appointed deputy U.S. marshal in Virgil's place. Marshal Dake agreed.

Ah, along with Morgan, were among the first men Wyatt deputized to assist him in pursuing Virgil's assassins. Others included "Turkey Creek" Jack Johnson, "Texas Jack" Vermillion, and Sherman McMasters, all competent men who would acquit themselves ably no matter the circumstances. Turkey Creek Jack was an old friend of Wyatt's from his Dodge City days. Ah can't say I knew more than who he was, though he was said to have bested two gamblers in a '76 shootout in Deadwood. Ah knew Texas Jack from Dodge and recommended him to Wyatt, a helpful addition as events would unfold. Sherm McMasters was a former Texas Ranger Wyatt and Ah knew from Dodge City. He came to Arizona from New Mexico in company of Cowboys Curly Bill Brocius and Pony Deal, though when trouble started, his sympathies turned our way.

January 17, 1882

Desert winter chill penetrates the bones. As ma condition worsened ma bones became more easily penetrated. Making ma way along Allen Street to the Alhambra, Ah huddled in ma great coat, seeking a bit of warmth. Ah did not notice the dandy, Cowboy scoundrel John Ringo exit the Oriental Saloon as Ah passed by.

"Well, lookey here, what do we have? I believe it's the lunger all bundled up like a squaw in a blanket."

Ah paused, giving thought to what Ah might do. Ah could ignore the provocation or acknowledge the inevitable. Ah chose the latter to foreclose giving any sign of weakness.

Ah turned. "Pardon me, suh. Is there some satisfaction you seek of me?"

"Satisfaction? I'll have none of your reb rabble honor. The only satisfaction I'll have of you is seeing you gunned down the way you killt Frank and Tom and Billy."

"They were murderous rustlers and scum. Same as you, Ringo. So, if you have the need, let's do it.

Ringo squared around to face me. Ah brushed back ma coat. Wyatt stepped out of the Oriental Saloon, inserting himself between us.

"Are you carrying, Ringo?"

"What's it to you, Earp? And what about him?"

"I'm a Deputy U.S. Marshal, Ringo."

"Ain't your jurisdiction. Now get out of

my way while I kill this blood-spittin' son-of-a-bitch."

"Saving your worthless life for the moment is my jurisdiction."

"It's *my* jurisdiction." City Marshal Dave Nagle announced his arrival. "Hand over the hardware. We're all goin' down to Recorder's Court."

"This ain't over, Lunger."

"It's not over," Wyatt said. "Not for anyone had a hand in shooting my brother. You have a deputy U.S. marshal's word on it."

Ringo spit on the boardwalk. Ringo and Ah paid our fines. The Deputy U.S. Marshal was not fined.

26

January 23, 1882

Wyatt persuaded justice Spicer to issue warrants for the arrests of Ike Clanton, Ike's brother Phin, and Pony Deal for the attempted murder of Virgil Earp. The charges were based on suspicion, strong in the case of Ike on account of the observation of witnesses at the scene, less so for the other two. We rode out intent to arrest them if we could, promising no quarter if they resisted. Ah had more confidence in the promise of no quarter than the prospect of arrest. Matters at hand had taken on the odor of blood-feud. With provocations having been exchanged, little doubt remained to the outcome.

Clanton Ranch

Late of a bright crisp morning we rode out to the Clanton ranch. The ranch house sat atop a low hill, a rambling adobe and stone affair with a commanding view of the San Pedro River valley below, not far from the town of Charleston. Wyatt drew a halt in a mesquite grove before coming into plain sight on the ranch road. Morgan, Turkey Creek Jack, and Ah drew up beside him.

"Looks quiet," Wyatt said.

"Does," Turkey Jack agreed.

"How you plan on playing this?" Ah asked.

Wyatt thought a moment. "Morg, circle around the base of the hill over yonder and come in from the rear just in case anyone tries to make a run for it. We'll give you a few minutes head start before we ride in."

Morg wheeled away. We waited, Wyatt marking the minutes by instinct. At some interval deemed timely, he led us out up the winding ranch road to the house on the hill. Ike sat on a front porch rocker eating a bowl of ice cream as we rode up. He set the dish aside to free his gun hand as we drew rein.

"You're trespassin'. Get off my land and take your refuse with you."

"Not trespassin', Ike. Official business. You're under arrest for the attempted murder of Tombstone city marshal, Virgil Earp."

Ike made a move toward his gun. He was greeted by Wyatt's drawn and cocked. "Two fingers, Ike. Ease it on out of that holster and drop it."

"On what authority?"

"Authority of this here warrant."

"You ain't no lawman."

"Deputy U.S. Marshal now. Get his gun, Jack."

Turkey Creek stepped down, picked up Ike's gun, and stuffed it in his belt.

"Where's Phin?"

"What do you want with Phin?"

"Got a warrant for him, too."

"He ain't here."

"Then I don't suppose you'll mind if Doc and Jack have a look around."

"No need," Morgan said coming around the corner from the back of the house, a sullen Phin Clanton at the point of his gun."

"Fair enough. Jack, see if you can find a couple of horses to get these two back to Tombstone."

Morgan and Turkey Creek took Ike and Phin into the city marshal's office in Tombstone. No sense taking a chance on Behan's lockup. Experience declared it an easy escape. Wyatt and Ah rode onto Charleston where we arrested Pony Deal without incident.

A preliminary hearing was held before Judge William H. Stilwell whereupon the defense produced a string of witnesses, all of whom swore to having seen the defendants in Charleston at the time of the shooting. Judge Stilwell dismissed all charges making it clear, no legal proceeding in Cochise County could be relied upon to bring Cowboy assassins to justice.

February 10, 1882
While the courts could not be relied upon to hold Ike Clanton and his Cowboy pals to account, Ike sought for a second time to have Wyatt, his brothers, and me once again charged with murder in the deaths of Billy Clanton and the McLaury brothers, this time before Justice of the Peace J.P. Smith in Contention. Warrants were issued February ninth. Johnny Behan arrested Wyatt, Morgan, and me on the tenth. We were to appear before Justice Smith in Contention in Behan's custody for the transfer. With Tom Fitch away at the time, we retained attorney William Herring to represent us. Wyatt sent word to Sherman McMasters who visited us in jail.

"You got a visitor," Behan announced, admitting McMasters to the cell block. "Let me know when you're finished," he said, locking the cell block door.

Sherm looked from Wyatt to Morgan to

me. "What the hell is going on here?"

"Ike," Wyatt said. "Found himself another court to try us in."

"Can he do that?"

"Justice Smith thinks he can."

"What can I do to help?"

"Behan's fixin' to take us to Contention tomorrow. I think it may be to set us up for an ambush."

"You want me and the boys to come along for the ride?"

"Might be best."

"Count on it."

Next morning, Behan led us out to a prison wagon. Don't know where he got it. Ah think the spectacle of Doc Holliday and the Earp brothers hauled off out of town as common criminals appealed to Behan's sense of self-importance. As he climbed into the box with his shotgun deputy, Sherm, Turkey Creek Johnson, and Texas Jack Vermillion rode up, armed with pistols and rifles.

"Where the hell do you think you're goin'?" Behan asked.

"Mornin', Sheriff." Sherm tipped his hat. "Along for the ride."

"You put them up to this, Earp?"

"Just doin' you the favor of a security guard, Johnny boy."

"I don't need a security guard."

"Don't suppose you do."

"Then why are they here?"

"In case we do."

With that, Behan laid lines on the mules. The road to Contention proved uneventful, as did the road back to Tombstone. Attorney Herring successfully argued Justice Smith's court was an inappropriate venue to hear charges brought and previously considered for events having occurred in Tombstone. Following some negotiation in the Justice's chamber, Justice Smith agreed to remand the case to Judge J.H. Lucas in Tombstone.

Judge Lucas heard testimony on behalf of the plaintiff consistent with that presented before Justice Spicer. Attorney Herring pointed out all of this had previously been considered at Justice Spicer's preliminary hearing and reviewed by the county grand jury who concurred with Justice Spicer's opinion in the matter. When asked if the prosecution had any new information to present, his request was respectfully declined. Judge Lucas, having determined no new information had come forward to justify reopening the proceedings, dismissed the charges.

It was now clear to all those with a stake in the feud, satisfaction would not be rendered at law. Lines were drawn. Neither side would back down. Events would unfold.

27

Campbell & Hatch Saloon and Billiard Parlor
March 18, 1882

The night of the treachery in question, Ah attended the theater in company of Morgan. After the performance Ah retired while Morg set off for a favored billiard parlor where he found Wyatt with Sherm McMasters. The proprietor, Bob Hatch, engaged Morg in billiard match at a table near the back of the saloon. As Morg bent over a rail shot, back windows of the saloon exploded in rifle fire. One shot narrowly missed Wyatt, another caught Morg in the back, dealing him a wound proved mortal. McMasters and Hatch ran to the alley from which the shots were fired but found only echoes of the assassins' footfalls running away. Medical attention could do nothing to save Morgan, who died at the scene, leaving Wyatt distraught and seared by a determined rage to the depths of a soul such as

Ah have never seen before or since.

A coroner's inquest convened the following morning. Pete Spencer's estranged wife came forward voluntarily in retaliation for her husband having beaten her. She named her husband, along with Frank Stilwell and a man called Indian Charlie as those responsible for planning and carrying out the attack. With Ike Clanton having been acquitted in the attempt on Virgil's life, the time for Tombstone law enforcement had passed. Wyatt resolutely took matters into his own hands, nominally as Deputy U.S. Marshal, for all the cover of respectability the badge might provide blood vengeance.

Ah observed a palpable change come over ma friend. Ah'd known him for a man of sober determination for all our acquaintanceship. This deepened to an iron-willed blood in his eye demand for vengeance nothing in nature could deny.

Contention City Depot
March 20, 1882
Ah accompanied Wyatt and his brothers James and Warren as they escorted Morgan's body to the depot for shipment to the family in California for burial. Virgil and his wife, Allie, would accompany the body on its journey. We were joined by Sherm Mc-

Masters and Turkey Creek Johnson, as none of us expected the threat of Cowboy violence had ended.

On reaching Contention, Wyatt received word by wire Cowboys awaited the Contention train in Tucson. Leaving our horses at the depot, we entrained in force to deal with whatever threat might be intended in Tucson.

We arrived in Tucson early that evening and took a bite of supper while waiting for the evening train bound for California to depart. After supper we walked to the depot to see Virgil and Allie safely aboard the train. It was then Wyatt spotted a man up the platform he took to be Frank Stilwell. Wyatt started for the man, who catching sight of Wyatt, jumped down from the platform and fled along the railbed. Wyatt gave chase. We followed.

Stilwell stumbled on the rough cinder roadbed and fell. He rolled on his back, coming up with a gun. Wyatt fired. James and Sherm backed his play with shots of their own. Ah turned ma gun on the depot evening shadows lest any other member of the Cowboy faction should seek to join the fray. None did.

The shooting attracted little immediate attention, Tucson being distracted by the ceremonial lighting of the city's first gas lights. The gunshots were taken for part of the celebratory revelry. Later discovery of the body would not.

With departure of the California westbound, we caught the evening freight to Contention City. Ah thought it a melancholy reminder of the last time Ah traveled by that conveyance. It was in company of Morgan the evening of October 25. So much had happened since that fateful night. So much more would come of this trip.

By this time the battle lines were well drawn. The Cowboys had opened a war on the Earp's and those aligned with them. Who shot Virgil? Who killed Morgan? It mattered little. We were all marked for murder. The Cowboys were united, and we were but ducks on a pond. Ducks on a pond have little recourse. We on the other hand had talons of our own.

We reached Contention City, collected our horses, and rode back to Tombstone.

Tombstone
Tuesday, March 21
Frank Stilwell's body was discovered early the next morning. Warrants were issued for our arrests on charges of murder as we were known to be in Tucson at the time of

Stilwell's death. Nothing more was needed to assume our guilt. While warrants made their way from Tucson to Tombstone, we prepared to ride out in search of others responsible for Morgan's murder. Leaving the Cosmopolitan Hotel, we were approached by Johnny Behan and two of his deputies.

"Wyatt, a word if I may."

Wyatt gave him a blue ice stare. "Ain't got time now, Johnny."

"Best make time. I got warrants out of Tucson for the arrest of the lot of you."

"On what charge?"

"The murder of Frank Stilwell."

"That'd be Bob Paul's jurisdiction. I'll see Bob in due course."

"I'm still the arresting officer in this jurisdiction."

"Sure, you are, Johnny. Sure, you are."

With that we mounted our horses and rode off leaving the paper tiger gaping in the street.

Wednesday, March 22

A search of Pete Spencer's logging camp revealed Pete, knowing we were looking for him, had gone to Tombstone and turned himself in to Behan's protective custody. There he was soon joined by Fred Bode.

We learned from the loggers Florentino Cruz, also known as Indian Charlie, was in the area. We had little difficulty finding Cruz.

Wyatt walked him up against a tree, pinning the cowering man there for questioning.

"Who killed Morgan?"

"I know nothing, *Señor* Wyatt."

"Too bad." Wyatt drew his gun. "Might have saved your sorry ass."

Round-eyed at the muzzle of the gun in his face, Indian Charlie spilled his guts.

"It was Ike put them up to it."

"Them *who*?"

"Please, *Señor* Wyatt. They will kill me."

"Not if I get to 'em first. And it don't matter much if I kill you now."

Hammer cocked, cylinder rolled and locked, deadly halo straight in the eye. Sweat lined Charlie's face. "Pete, Frank Stilwell, Curly Bill, John Ringo, Fred Bode, Hank Swilling."

Wyatt eased off the hammer. "Long list."

Charlie relaxed. "Ike, he was plenty mad. Said no Cowboy would know any peace as long as the Earps was alive."

"Why would you go along with such a thing? What did my brothers and I ever do to you?"

He shrugged. "These men, they are my friends."

"For that you let them gun down my brother? He was my *brother,* you know."

"What could I do?"

"I'll show you what you could do." He emptied his gun into the round-eyed body of Florentino Cruz. Another murder warrant would be issued this time in Johnny Behan's jurisdiction.

We learned Sheriff Behan meant to have us brought to law, though he lacked the stomach and skill to accomplish such a thing. He rounded up a posse — a Cowboy posse — to legalize their plan to kill us all. His gang of cutthroats included John Ringo, Curly Bill Brocius, Phin Clanton and others named by Indian Charlie in the plot to murder Morgan and Wyatt.

Knowing we were being pursued and knowing the whereabouts of our pursuers were two different things. We headed out to rough country planning to hideout and see what we might learn of Behan's next move while giving some thought to our own. Wyatt knew a place we might camp affording water and cover.

■ ■ ■ ■

Riding into Iron Springs early in the morning where we intended to rest and water our horses, we were ambushed. Members of Behan's posse under the leadership of Curly Bill Brocius, were camped in the wash bordering the springs. The first volley of gunfire shot Texas Jack's horse out from under him. He ducked behind the animal trying to draw his Winchester from the saddle boot pinned under the horse. Outnumbered and surprised, we scattered for cover. On seeing Texas Jack pinned down, Ah rode back to pick him up. Wyatt, as Wyatt was wont to do, dropped from his horse and returned fire. Recognizing Curly Bill among the attackers, Wyatt cut loose a shotgun blast that felled the gang leader as Texas Jack and Ah reached cover.

Having withdrawn to the shelter of a nearby grove of trees, Sherm, Texas Jack, Turkey Creek, and Ah laid down covering fire for Wyatt, who now drew full fury of the Cowboy assault. With our attackers pinned down by covering fire, Wyatt managed to collect his spooked horse, mount, and retreat to the trees.

With Curly Bill down, the Cowboys had no stomach to fight it out with us. They threw Curly Bill's body across the back of a horse and rode off. Satisfied the Cowboys weren't coming back, we left the cover of the trees. We watered our horses as planned but did not risk tarrying long at the springs.

In need of supplies and fresh horses, we had no choice but to go into hiding, while Behan's men combed the countryside searching for us. We found refuge at Harry Hooker's Sierra Bonita Ranch. Harry proved willing to shelter us at the risk of his own person and property, providing the fresh horses and supplies we needed.

28

Hotel Glenwood
Glenwood Springs, Colorado
October 1887

Ah must have dozed off. Ah awoke with a start. Black silence. Ah thought perhaps . . .

Cugh, cugh, cugh . . . iron taste. Blood. Not yet.

Ah sat up, sensing a presence. Lurking there in the shadows. A horse stomped, impatient. *You shall have to wait. Ah shall not gratify you just yet.* Of that, how could Ah be sure? Ah heard a sound, as if a chuckle. Cold chilled a shiver. Could it be Ah converse with Perdition himself? *Be gone, scallywag, be gone!*

Ah fumbled for a lucifer, irony that. Scratched to light. The bedside lamp bloomed. Ah trimmed the wick. Better. The four corners stood shrouded in shadow, bereft of deathly spirit. Kate's chair stood by the bedside table empty. Dear Kate, angel of mercy. Surely, she did not think herself such, though she was. More than Ah deserved for all ma ill-treatment of her lo these many years. All come to this. Blood stained the front of ma nightshirt.

Ah lay back to stare into the gloom.

Presently, footfalls sounded in the corridor. The door latch announced her return.

Sierra Bonita
March 27

Harry Hooker was Wyatt's friend, a wealthy rancher, and no fan of Cowboy rustlers. We spent a restful evening, though our respite was not to last long. The following morning, lookouts spotted a large band of riders approaching from the southwest. It had to be Behan and his posse. Hooker's ranch compound amounted to a fortress built to withstand the threat of Apache raids. He offered to help us make a stand there. Wyatt thanked him for his offer and all the help already given but declined to further entangle him in troubles with what passed for the law.

Slipping out the back of the compound, we rode into the foothills of nearby mountains and took up defensive positions. With the advantage of high ground, we resolved to have it out with Behan and his Cowboy band. We watched Behan and his men enter Sierra Bonita. We watched them leave, riding off in the direction of Fort Grant. A misdirection likely owed to Harry Hooker's hospitality. We spent a quiet night, complete with the comforts of a campfire.

Behan and his men returned to the area the next morning. They rode around aimlessly, searching nooks and crannies in a fruitless attempt to find us. Hiding in plain sight, a schoolboy might have tracked us, but not Johnny Behan. By midday, the posse rode southwest, returning to Tombstone, failed as ever Sheriff Behan failed.

We left the hilltop and returned to Sierra Bonita to consider where next to proceed. Ah caught up with Wyatt after supper, taking the evening air from the ranch headquarters wall. The valley stretched blue and purple haze to the horizon where a pale moon rose spectral over the eastern foothills.

Cugh, cugh . . . disease gave ma presence away.

"Ain't gonna sneak up on anybody that way, Doc."

"Expect Ah'll have to shoot first and sneak later. Now what?"

"Good question. One I been chewin' on some myself."

"And?"

"Don't like unfinished business."

"Unfinished?"

"Ringo, for one."

"He worth it?"

"If it was just Behan, it might be worth a try. He can't find his ass with both hands in broad daylight. Problem is, he'll have the whole damn territory huntin' us. The U.S. Marshal play only goes so far. Some might say we've gone too far already."

"After all our experiences with Arizona law, we might be tempting fate to risk another run through the courts at that."

"Might at that."

We fell silent for a long time to a pair of hoot owls in heat and a lonely coyote.

"Quickest way out of Arizona is by way of New Mexico," he said, thinking out loud. "Deming's nearest railhead. From there a man can get good and lost."

With thanks to Harry, we rode out next morning.

Deming
New Mexico Territory
In Deming we caught up to another problem. Money. We sold the horses Harry Hooker gave us to pay fare and food to get us as far as Albuquerque. Ah could see the wheels turning in Wyatt's brain as moun-

tains rolled by dust-stained coach windows on the ride north. Ah figured he'd think of something.

"When do you figure to head to San Francisco?"

He glanced away from the window, brow raised. "San Francisco?"

"Where she went, is it not?"

"Josephine?"

"Who else?"

"Got me all figured have you, Doc?"

"You read like an open book, Wyatt."

"S'pose I do. I'll not deny, I've thought about it."

"Sure, you have. Now when do you plan on leaving?"

"When the time is right. Since it is clearly the hour of prying time, what are you planning to do?"

"Gamble till Ah die."

"That's it?"

Cugh . . . cugh, cugh . . . cugh. "What more can there be for me?" What more indeed?

"There are places take care of those in your condition."

"You mean a pest house? Now you sound like Kate. No way in hell."

"Can't have that."

"Hell?"

"No. Sounding like Kate."

■ ■ ■ ■

Albuquerque
New Mexico Territory

Soon after we arrived in Albuquerque, Wyatt located Frank McLane, an old friend from Dodge City. McLane was somewhat aware of our situation having followed sketchy newspaper accounts of events taking place in Tombstone. He put us up while we caught some much needed rest. Wyatt filled him in on the events of the gunfight, trial, Virgil's ambush, Morgan's assassination, and our pursuit of those responsible. He sat beside a crackling mesquite fire, our chairs drawn up around the fireplace.

"Quite a story, Wyatt. What do you plan to do now?"

"Not sure, exactly. We need to put more distance between us and Behan's gunmen."

"How can I help?"

"Putting us up here is a big help already, Frank."

"Least I can do. How are you fixed for traveling money?"

Wyatt paused, uncomfortable with the question.

McLane continued with his own answer. "Tapped out, is it?"

Wyatt nodded.

"Tell you what, how about I swing you a loan? Say two thousand. Would that help?"

"Be a big help. Got to tell you, though, I don't know when I might be able to repay you."

"You will when you can. I'll see about it come morning."

A week later, we bid Frank our thanks and entrained northbound for Colorado. The only thing Colorado had to recommend it is the distance it put between us and Tombstone. Ah could find gaming action to ma liking anywhere. Wyatt, for his part, could wrestle with the lingering demons from Morgan's death wherever he found himself beyond the reach of Behan and the Cowboy cutthroats he rode with.

Trinidad, Colorado

Upon our arrival in Trinidad, Wyatt led us to the city marshal's office. Ah thought it unwise as we remained fugitives. Wyatt knew best. We found the city marshal in.

"Wyatt Earp. Well, I declare. Come to turn yourself in?"

"Nice to see you too, Bat."

We shook hands all around. Bat checked the clock on the wall.

"Four-thirty. Close enough for supper and

a couple of beers. What do you say?"

"Best offer I've had on train fare for the last two days," Wyatt said.

"Sanbourn's is around the corner. Food's good, and it's quiet. You boys won't attract so much attention there."

We took a corner table, the saloon all but deserted at this early hour. Beers were ordered along with the roast beef special. Ah requested whiskey.

"Been reading a lot about you boys," Bat said as the beers were served.

"Wanted dodgers?" Sherm asked.

"In the stack. No, newspaper accounts, sketchy at best. What's the truth of it?"

Wyatt took up the story. "All began with that Benson stage holdup, you may recall."

Bat nodded. "Rode with the posse. Nabbed one, as I recall. Fella named King. You ever get the rest of 'em?"

"Not so you could pin a conviction on any of them. The Cowboys could put up witnesses willing to testify the accused were anywhere but there faster than Lady Justice could swear them in. Local law took that 'Justice is blind' notion to where the lady couldn't find the outhouse for fallin' in it."

"Behan?"

"Who else? If there was shit to be found, you can bet Behan was there steppin' in it."

"Not surprised."

The waiter arrived with the first servings. With seven of us, it took two whiskies worth to finish the job. He may have brought the bottle.

"Deck was stacked against us," Wyatt continued. "Ike Clanton and Behan tried to pin the robbery on Doc, me, Morgan, and Virgil."

"Ambitious lie where a city and U.S. marshal is accused."

"Lyin' might be the best thing Behan is suited for. He sure wanted no part of facing me in the next election. Pinning attempted robbery and murder on the lot of us seemed like the best way around that showdown."

"No surprise there, either. That cause the shootout?"

"Not directly. That was mostly Ike's doing."

"Ike who lived to tell about it?"

"That's the one."

Events leading up to the gunfight hadn't been widely reported. Wyatt recounted them for Bat before concluding.

"When Virg was ambushed and Morg murdered, the lines were drawn. I got myself appointed Deputy U.S. Marshal in Virgil's stead and deputized these men. Went after the murderers with proper warrants."

"Any arrests?" Bat asked with a smirk.

Wyatt met his gaze with a raised brow. "One. He tried to escape."

"That's a different story than the one circulating out of Tombstone."

" 'Course it is. That one is the Cowboy version as told by Behan."

"Well, you've come to the right place."

"How's that?"

"I haven't seen hide nor hair of any of you, though I'd advise getting out of town before anybody else does."

Further to Bat's good advice we split up, disguising any trail of pursuit. McMasters and Johnson headed west. Jack Vermillion followed his roots back to Virginia. Wyatt and his brother hid out near Gunnison Colorado. Ah boarded the Denver & Rio Grande to Pueblo. Perhaps not the wisest of choices as events would unfold.

29

Pueblo
May 1882

Bat may have been wise to advise leaving town before anyone noticed our presence, though for ma part, Ah must have attracted some notice. Early one evening not long after arriving in Pueblo, Ah went to the Birdcage Comique and Saloon in search of a game. There Ah was approached by a man theretofore unknown to me.

"Doc. Doc Holliday."

He was a man of diminutive stature and shabby attire. "Suh, Ah believe you have the advantage of me."

"Perry, Perry Mallon. You saved my life down to Santa Fe."

Never having been in Santa Fe, Ah took it for a mistaken identity. Before Ah could right the misunderstanding, he continued. "Time to repay the favor."

Curious now. "And what would that be?"

"Frank Stilwell's brother is in town looking for you."

"Are you sure of this?"

"He inquired as to my having seen you."

"You know him, then."

"From my time in Lincoln, New Mexico."

"Ah see. What did you tell him?"

"Said I had no idea where you might be."

"Ah thank you for that. We shall call your debt square."

With that, he tipped his cap and drifted off in the crowd.

A week later, Masterson sent a wire proposing we attend horse races scheduled for the following week in Denver. Ah boarded the Denver train the next week, joining Bat and two of his friends from Pueblo. We took lodging at the Windsor Hotel.

Windsor Hotel
Denver

With three hundred guest rooms, the Windsor could only be described as opulent. Furnished in polished wood, red velvet, and marble with a massive bar, crystal chandeliers and oriental art.

On the eve of the races as Ah returned to the hotel after dinner, Ah was stopped on the street by Arapahoe county sheriff's deputies in the company of the man Ah knew as Perry Mallon. Mallon now represented himself as a deputy sheriff, having a Cochise County warrant for my arrest. The deputies informed me Ah was under arrest for the murder of Frank Stilwell. They handcuffed me and led me to jail.

The warrant, of course, bore the odor of Johnny Behan about it. Stilwell having met his demise in Pima County, Behan would have no jurisdiction. Extradition to Cochise County under force of such an order amounted to a death warrant. Fortunately, newspapers took interest in my plight. Some flogged Mallon's lies, but most gave me fair hearing in the court of public opinion. Sufficient attention was drawn to my predicament and the dubious provenance of the warrant for ma arrest as to be of some benefit to me.

City Marshal's Office
Trinidad, Colorado
News of my incarceration reached Wyatt, who sought out Bat Masterson to see what might be done to assist me. The office door swung open to Bat at his desk.

"Mornin', Bat."

"Morning, Wyatt. What brings you back this way?"

"Doc's in trouble."

272

"Read something about that. Likely explains why he never showed up for the races."

"Races?"

"We went up to Denver couple of weeks ago to try a wager on the ponies racing there. Doc never showed up for the races. Doc being Doc, I never thought too much of it until I read the newspaper accounts. Sounds like Behan's got a collar on him."

"More than a collar. They extradite him to Cochise County, Doc's a dead man."

"He already is."

"Not that way. Behan's got no jurisdiction in the Stilwell case. Frank met his maker in Pima County. That's Bob Paul's jurisdiction."

"You figure to get Doc out of this?"

"I can't. If I show my face anywhere near there, I'll be sittin' in the cell next to Doc."

"I see."

"That's why I'm here, Bat. To see if you can figure a way to head this off. I know you sort of put up with Doc on account of our friendship, but he don't deserve what Behan has in store for him."

"No, probably not. Seeing it's you asking, maybe two can play this jurisdiction game."

■ ■ ■ ■

City Marshal's Office
Pueblo, Colorado

City Marshal Angus Jamieson finished his rounds on a bright sunny morning ready for a second cup of coffee. Returning to his office, he found a visitor waiting.

"Bat Masterson, what brings you to Pueblo?"

"Professional courtesy, Angus."

"Well, that sure sounds like business. How about a cup of coffee to get things started?"

"Suits me."

Jamieson pulled two tin cups from a cupboard next to the potbelly stove. He poured two steaming cups, set one at his desk guest chair for Bat and took his seat. He took a sip.

"That's better. Now what's this professional courtesy all about?"

"Need you to issue an arrest warrant for Doc Holliday."

"Hellfire, man, don't you read the papers? They already got him arrested up in Denver. Murder charge to boot."

"Forget the Cochise County arrest warrant. It's a death sentence, sure as we're sitting here."

"Murder most often is."

"If there's a fair trial, the defendant found guilty by a jury and so judged by sentencing. Trust me when I tell you this isn't that kind of warrant. This warrant sees the accused extradited and assassinated before he ever sees inside of a courtroom."

"Then you best tell me about it."

"The warrant Doc is being held on was issued in Cochise County for a murder occurred in Pima County."

"Odd. Why so?"

"You could call it a blood feud between Wyatt Earp, his brothers, and the outlaw faction known as the Cowboys."

"What's that got to do with Holliday?"

"Doc rode with Wyatt when they went after Cowboys responsible for murdering Wyatt's brother Morgan and near killing his older brother Virgil."

"Outlaws ain't generally given to handing out arrest warrants. How does that come about?"

"Crooked sheriff in the Cowboys pocket. Can you help me, Angus?"

"Hmm. . . ." He drummed his fingers on his desk. "Now that I think about it, Doc *did* leave a little unfinished business here in Pueblo."

■ ■ ■

Turned out ma failure to return to Pueblo from Denver created certain financial obligations Ah had failed to make good on with regard to hotel accommodations, an unpaid gambling marker, and a weapons charge overlooked in the serving.

Sheriff's Office
Denver

Bat arrived in Denver along with Marshal Jamieson and a warrant for ma arrest. Bat left the serving of the warrant to Jamieson as his association with Wyatt and me were certain to cast suspicion on the charges.

"Sheriff Spangler, Angus Jamieson, City Marshal in Pueblo."

"Marshal, what can I do for you?"

"I have a warrant here for the arrest of Doc Holliday. I understand you are currently holding him on an Arizona charge."

"We are. What's he done this time?"

Jamieson handed over the warrant for Spangler to inspect the charges. Spangler handed the warrant back. "I'll not turn him over on misdemeanors. A murder charge takes precedent."

"Now see here, Sheriff, local jurisdiction

certainly has prior claim."

"Neither claim is in my county. My county, my call."

"Neither of us decide jurisdiction."

"Take it to a judge. Good day, Marshal."

30

While all this took place, Behan kept to his
old tricks, petitioning Arizona Governor F. A. Tritle to request ma extradition to
Cochise County. The governor refused, cit-
ing lack of jurisdiction. Behan then turned
to Pima County Sheriff Bob Paul with a
request to issue a warrant for the murder of
Frank Stilwell and pursue my extradition to
Pima County. This Paul agreed to do,
though he must have known the Cowboys
had other plans for me than a fair trial by a
jury of ma peers. A fair man, Sheriff Paul
undertook extradition personally, Governor
Tritle being more sympathetic to Pima
County's claim of jurisdiction.

Arapaho County Jail
Denver
The jailer opened the cellblock door to the
whine of hinges in need of oil in the tawny
light of late afternoon.

"You have a visitor, Holliday. Knock when you're finished," he said as Bat Masterson entered the block. The noisy door closed with a heavy clank. Bat walked to my cell and pulled up a visitor chair.

"Doc."

"Bat. Good of you to come."

"Wyatt sent me."

"Ah, Wyatt." *Cugh . . . cugh.* "He . . . would."

"They treating you all right?"

"Not the Windsor Hotel as you can see."

"I see that. We missed you at the races."

"Ah was regrettably detained."

"I can see that too. We'll do our best to get you out of here."

"Ah'd much appreciate that."

"Marshal Jamieson from Pueblo presented a warrant for your arrest."

"Oh? What did I do now?"

"Misdemeanors. Just enough to get you into a more favorable custody situation."

"And?"

"Sheriff Spangler won't honor the warrant. Claims murder is the more pressing charge."

"Does he get to decide that?"

"No. Court does, though in this case the jurisdictions in dispute are territorial. Likely end up in the governor's office."

"What's to be done about that?"

"Don't know yet. Working on it, though."

Sheriff's Office
Denver

On his arrival in Denver, Pima County Sheriff Bob Paul called on Sheriff Spangler with his warrant for ma transfer to Pima County to answer for the charge of Frank Stilwell's murder.

Spangler looked over the order shaking his head. "Like I told Mallon, you need the governor to request extradition. An arrest warrant gets the man held. It doesn't get him transferred to another territory."

"Who's Mallon?"

"The arresting officer. One of Sheriff Behan's deputies. Don't you people down there talk to each other?"

"We do. That's why I'm here."

"Well, come on back when you have a court order honoring the Arizona governor's extradition request."

Spangler delayed proceedings pending receipt of Governor Tritle's request. The delay served to ma advantage. Bat came by soon after to see to ma condition. Ah explained the situation.

"So, we have a little time," he said, fingering his moustache.

"It would appear so, but what is to be done with it?"

"Governor Tritle's request must first go to Colorado Governor Pitkin. He can ask a court to honor the request or refuse it outright himself. Pitkin is the key. All we have to do is persuade him to honor Marshal Jamieson's warrant."

"That's all, is it? How you figure to do that?"

"Haven't figured that part out yet. For a starter, I need a meeting with him."

"You don't just drop in on a governor."

"No, I suppose you don't. Need to figure that one out, too — though just maybe. . . ."

It didn't take Bat long to figure things out. He returned to visit the next day.

"Figured all that out so soon?"

"May have. I called at the governor's office."

"You got to see him?"

"Oh, no. He's away on business. Won't return to the office until day after tomorrow."

Ah winced. *Cugh, cugh, cugh.* "How long do you suppose it will take Bob Paul to get Tritle's extradition request?"

"Chances are Bob's waiting at the governor's office when he returns."

"Ah was afraid of that."

"All we have to do is get to the governor before he gets to the office."

"How are you fixing to do that?"

"He returns to Denver tomorrow. I'll pay him a visit at the governor's mansion tomorrow night."

"Just like that? Why, likely he invites you to dinner. How you going to arrange that?"

"Trevor Cowen."

"And who might that be?"

"A reporter for the *Denver Tribune*. He's an old friend. Covers the capital and is well known to Governor Pitkin. He tells me the governor will see him on an urgent matter of life and death."

"Is that. Ah hope this works."

"So do I."

Governor's Mansion
May 28
8 P.M.

Cowen didn't get Bat invited to the governor's dinner table, but they did manage to interrupt his after-dinner brandy and cigar.

"The governor will see you now." The butler showed them into the dining room where Governor Pitkin had just finished his supper.

"This had better be good, Trevor. Matters of life and death at this hour after a long day's travel are hard on the digestion. Who do we have here?"

"Good evening, Governor, and thank you for seeing us on such irregular terms. This is W.B. Masterson, city marshal in Trinidad, formerly of Dodge City, Kansas."

"Bat Masterson. Your reputation precedes you, sir."

"Comes in handy once in a while, and again, thank you for seeing us, Governor."

"What can I do for you?"

"I'm here on behalf of John Henry Holliday who is currently being held in the Arapaho County jail."

"Yes, something about an Arizona murder charge as I recall reading in the papers. I suppose Arizona wants him extradited."

"We believe a request is forthcoming. John Henry is also subject of warrants for his arrest in Pueblo. Sheriff Spengler refuses to turn him over to Pueblo authorities."

"Didn't Trevor say you are marshal in Trinidad? What have you got to do with Pueblo?"

"I came on Marshal Jamieson's behalf, as I am knowledgeable of the situation in Tombstone."

"Tombstone, is it? Now I'm confused."

"The extradition request, should you receive it, will be to face charges in Pima

County, but lawless elements in Cochise County and Tombstone are behind the request. They have no interest in seeing John Henry receive a fair trial."

"We can stop with the John Henry. I know who Doc Holliday is."

"The short of it is extradition is a death sentence. Doc will never see the inside of a court room."

"So, what do you want me to do?"

"Honor the Pueblo arrest warrant."

"Let me sleep on it. We'll put it before Judge Elliot in the morning."

Arapaho County Courthouse
May 29

Sheriff Spangler took me in custody to a court hearing with respect to the jurisdictional claims against me. Bat was present along with Pueblo Marshal Jamieson. Pima County Arizona Sheriff Bob Paul was there having delivered Arizona Governor Tritle's request for ma extradition to Governor Pitkin's office that morning. Governor Pitkin, who would decide the extradition question, was also present.

"All rise. Arapaho County Court is now in session, the honorable Ezra Elliot presiding."

The Judge took his seat at the bench,

motioning all of us to take our seats. "Governor Pitkin, I believe you have a decision to place before this court in the matter of an Arizona Territorial request for extradition of John Henry Holliday to face capital murder charges with respect to the murder of one," — he checked the order before him — "Frank Stilwell."

The governor rose. "I have, Your Honor. I have examined Governor Tritle's request and find it defective in form. I therefore respectfully place the matter of the Pueblo Colorado arrest warrant before the court."

Sheriff Spangler turned scarlet, though to his credit, he held his tongue. Bob Paul's jaw dropped.

"This court then orders the accused, John Henry Holliday, remanded to custody of Pueblo City Marshal Angus Jamieson."

With that, Sheriff Spangler released me to the custody of Marshal Jamieson. Leaving the courtroom, Bob Paul approached us.

"Bat."

"Bob."

"What the hell are you doing here, if I might ask?"

"Favor for a friend."

"I can figure who that might be. How'd you pull that off?" he said tossing his head back toward the bench.

"You're a good man, Bob. Doing your job. You know as well as I do, once back in Arizona, Doc, here, would never see the inside of a courtroom. Behan and his Cowboy pals would see to that."

"I know. That's why I came personally to see justice done proper."

"For what it's worth, Doc didn't kill Stilwell. Justice is better served this way."

"Guilt or innocence is best left to a judge and jury."

"True, Bob. Do you really think there is a judge and jury between Doc and his would-be executioners?"

"No. I suppose you're right. Justice is better served this way. Just don't tell anyone I said so."

With that we took our leave. Bat accompanied Marshal Jamieson and me back to Pueblo. On reaching Pueblo, the case against me was continued to July, and Ah was released on bail.

31

Gunnison, Colorado
June 16, 1882

With ma presence in Pueblo known to Behan and the Cowboy faction, Ah quietly boarded a westbound stage to join Wyatt in Gunnison. If a man needed a place to hideout, Gunnison had much to recommend it. Remote, isolated, and quiet. Miners mined some gold, though not a gold rush boomtown. Ranchers did business in cattle, and farmers did business in farming. Prosperous and civil. What better place could men wanted for murder find to hideout?

Arriving in town, after but a few inquiries, Ah learned that Wyatt and his younger brother Warren just happened to be in residence at Wentworth's Boardinghouse.

"Doc, thought you might come our way if Bat got you out of that little jam. Glad you did."

"That little jam you refer to had three law enforcement jurisdictions and two governors tussling over the privilege of incarcerating ma bones if not hanging them."

"Notorious fellow such as yourself, I'm not surprised."

"You're not surprised. I wasn't amused. You sent the right man for the job, though. Ah don't suppose Masterson volunteered to come to ma aid out of any deep affection he may hold for me. Ah thank you for your part in persuading him to do that."

"Friends look after friends. I'd have come myself if I could have without ending up in the same bind as you. How'd Bat pull it off?"

"Managed to head off Bob Paul and Arizona Governor Tritle by beating them to Governor Pitkin's dinner table. Bat convinced him ma Pueblo misdemeanors carried more weight than an Arizona murder warrant."

"I swear that man could talk the balls off a brass monkey if he was a mind to."

"Ah'm inclined to agree, though Ah'm no judge of brass monkeys, never mind attachments to their nethers."

"Well, you're here, and that brings me to unfinished business."

Cugh, cugh . . . cugh. "Ringo."

"That's what I like about you, Doc. We may be different, but we think alike."

"What do you propose?"

"Kill the son-of-a-bitch."

"Ah might have guessed as much. Have you more of a plan than that?"

"I have."

Four days later we boarded the D&RG southbound for Deming by way of Santa Fe and Albuquerque.

Deming, New Mexico

We paused our journey to refresh ourselves in Deming, taking a room at the Commercial Hotel. Over supper we discussed the way ahead.

"How do you propose to find Ringo? We are not exactly unknown to his friends and haunts. If we go looking for him, he will surely hear of it."

"I have been giving that some thought. Our friend Sherm McMasters rode with the Cowboys some. You had some bad blood with Ringo, too, as I recall."

"Ah'm listening."

"So, what if Sherm warns Ringo he's seen you in, say Galeyville, and you're out for John Ringo's blood?"

"Sherm isn't here."

"You know that, and I know that. Ringo

doesn't know that."

"Why Galeyville?"

"To get there, Ringo's got to come through the Dragoon Mountain's south pass."

"Ah see," Ah said lifting ma glass. "You, suh, are a devious bastard, Wyatt Earp."

"You flatter me."

We boarded the Southern Pacific west from Deming to Lordsburg. There we obtained horses and supplies for the trail. From Lordsburg we entered Cochise County unknown to anyone. We rode into Galeyville where a telegram signed Sherman McMasters was sent to Johnny Ringo in Tombstone warning Ringo of ma presence in Galeyville and ma designs on having ma satisfaction of him.

From Galeyville we rode west to the south pass of the Dragoon Mountains. We found a cave on the heights above the pass with good visibility of the trail coming east. There we set about to wait. Hot. Hotter than a two-dollar whore on Saturday night. Dry wind laced with burning sand added to misery. The cave did little to staunch the heat, though the walls of the oven took the worst of the sun. Ah began to wonder who might perish by this vendetta.

■ ■ ■ ■

Dragoon Mountains
South Pass
July 13, 1882

Ah thought at first it might be a mirage growing out of the heat shimmer. A speck, at first, it grew, resolving into the silhouette of a horse and rider.

"Look there," Ah said. "Someone's coming."

We watched.

"It's him," Wyatt said at length.

As he drew closer, Ah noticed unsteady posture. "Having some acquaintance with the condition, Ah do believe he's drunk."

Wyatt descended through the rocks to a position beside the trail. As Ringo reached his place of concealment, he stepped out, gun drawn.

"Lift your hands, Ringo."

"I declare, Wyatt Earp. What are you doin' here?"

"Waitin' for you. Now drop that gun, two fingers, nice and easy."

Ringo did, as Warren and Ah made our way to Wyatt's side.

"You, too, Holliday. You're the one I come for. Not surprised you felt the need of help."

"Shut up, Ringo," Wyatt said. "Now, step down."

This he did while Warren took the horse's leads.

"Take off your boots."

"My boots. What for?"

"You're goin' for a walk."

"A walk he says. A walk. You're gonna kill me. I die here as good as anywhere else."

"Who says I'm gonna kill you? Now take off them boots."

Ringo sat on a rock and pulled off his boots while Ah covered him. Wyatt picked up Ringo's gun and stuffed it in his belt. He took Ringo's horse from Warren who went to fetch ours. Wyatt tied Ringo's boots to his horse's saddle. We mounted.

"All right, Johnny. As I recall, you were headed for Galeyville. Lead on."

Ringo walked. We rode. The sun beat down hammer on anvil, ringing in shimmers of heat haze.

"My feet are getting cut up on these rocks."

"Shut up and keep walkin'."

"I'm dyin' of thirst."

"Shut up and keep walkin'."

Five or so miles out of Galeyville, Wyatt drew a halt. North of the trail a lone Sissoo tree stood. "Feel like a little shade, Johnny?"

"Gonna kill me here?"

"Who says I'm gonna kill you?"

"Me, you son-of-a-bitch."

"Head on over to that tree yonder and give some thought to back-shootin' a man playin' billiards."

"Hell's bells, a tree."

"Good a place as any, Johnny. And if those are hell's bells, I do believe they ring for ye."

Ah smiled to ma-self. Poetic of all things. We reached the tree.

"Have a seat, Johnny. Make yourself nice and comfortable.

Ringo sat. Wyatt stepped up beside him, drew Ringo's gun from his belt, leveling it aside Ringo's right temple. Ringo jerked at the sound of the hammer cock.

"Shame about that, Johnny."

"Shame about you killin' me?"

"Shame about you killin' yourself before I had a chance." He fired.

Ringo's horse bolted into the desert. We propped the body up against the tree and enclosed Ringo's gun in the dead man's hand.

"I wasn't going to kill you, Johnny. You were going to do it all along. Now maybe Morg can rest easy with them bells ringin' for you."

He propped Ringo's rifle against a nearby rock. We stepped into our saddles and rode back the way we came.

32

Hotel Glenwood
Glenwood Springs, Colorado
October 1887

Kate glanced out the window. Golden light lengthening in shadow. She shook her head.

"What troubles you?"

She lifted a brow. "You know very well. All the killin' and trouble followed the Earps like their own shadow and you right with them."

"Ma friends, Kate. What was Ah to do?"

"Spend your days in peace with me in Globe. But no. That wouldn't do, would it? Look where it got us. Look where it got you. Two lives. . . ."

"There, there. Now we have here." *Cugh, cugh, cugh, cugh.*

"Sure, we do. Listen to you."

She wiped at ma chin with fresh linen. "You are an angel of mercy, my darlin'."

"Maybe I am, for one brief spell in this

life, though you damn sure know it ain't by choice."

"Ah know that and Ah love you all the more for it."

She rose. "Now get some rest."

Ah closed ma eyes. The door latch clicked her departure. Nearby a horse nickered.

Board Of Trade Saloon
Leadville, Colorado
July 1882

After righting the matter of Johnny Ringo, Ah followed Lady Luck to Leadville. Upon ma arrival in Leadville, Ah determined to become a model citizen of upright demeanor and proper decorum starting with the Leadville ordinance prohibiting the carrying of firearms in town. Going about unheeled, Ah scrupulously avoided troublesome situations and so doing lived peaceably, despite disease tightening its relentless grip on ma lungs.

The town boomed out of a silver strike in the '70s. Silver production petered out by the onset of the '80s, but boom town gaming and vice remained strong. Ah took to the tables in various of the more than one hundred gaming establishments along Harrison Avenue, among them John Morgan's Board of Trade saloon. Ah took residence in

Mannie Hyman's saloon, occasionally dealing faro there.

Cugh, cugh, cugh . . . cugh.

Ah poured another drink in hopes whiskey
would quench the fire in ma chest or at least
render me dull to its effects.

"Doc, that stuff ain't helpin' none."

John Morgan, ever solicitous of ma health.
"Consumption no, consumption some, ma
friend." Ah poured another drink.

"Been to the doctor lately?"

"To what good?"

"Maybe he could prescribe something to
ease the cough. Whiskey sure ain't helpin'."

Laudanum Ah thought to ma self-
diagnosis. *Perhaps, couldn't hurt to give it a
try.* "Thank you, John, I shall take you up
on your advice."

Ah can't say the laudanum helped. It
certainly did not hurt, though when mixed
with whiskey, which Ah continued to con-
sume, one had to strike a balance to remain
competitive at the tables. Ah survived the
fog of disease, managing to stay ahead of
the horseman for the next two years.

Hyman's Saloon
July 1884
Ma conditioned worsened in spite of the
opium elixir better serving ma tolerance to

discomfort. Better, though dull comfort did little to slack my thirst. It served to fortify ma drinking. As things progressed John may have come to regret his medicinal advice. Ah accepted as inevitable the rider's pursuit.

To ma condition, Lady Luck added insult to infirmity. She deserted ma game. She is a fickle wench, though some speculate medications may have played a part in the deleterious decline of ma acumen at the tables. Ah placed no store by such notions. The faithless whore to fortune was not to be trusted. Perhaps such thinking further offended her, for she tripped me with yet another pair of tricks when two disreputable characters from ma Tombstone past found their way into town.

Johnny Tyler, with whom Ah had contentious relations during ma time at the Oriental dealing in Wyatt's concession along with former Ike Clanton Cowboy, Billy Allen. Tyler came into Hyman's saloon one evening backed by rowdy cronies he sought to impress with bravado directed to ma person. I sat at ma usual corner table, medicating ma dissipation with whiskey.

"There he sits boys, Doc Holliday, the Cowboy killer himself. Killed any Cowboys lately, Doc? No, I suppose not. No Earp to hide behind here."

"Ah, Johnny Tyler. No, no Earp here, for if there were, you'd surely tuck your scallywag tail between your bowed legs and slink out of town."

"Big talk for a scrawny lunger a stiff breeze might blow away. Now, if you was to back up your palaver, you'd pull so I could return the favor of your killin' my friends."

Ah laid ma hands on the table. "Not armed, Johnny. You must know there's an ordinance against carrying firearms in Leadville."

"Listen to him, boys. Doc Holliday's become a law-abiding citizen. Goes right nice with the yellow streak down his back, don't yah think?"

With that, Ah stood and turned to the stairs to go to ma room.

"Look there, boys, he turns tail and runs, yellow streak and all."

"Ah should bide ma tongue if Ah were you, Johnny. One never knows when one might have to eat it."

"That a threat, Doc? If it is, get yourself heeled and back it up."

Ah climbed the stairs.

"Yellow son-of-a-bitch."

Ah found the incident an embarrassing insult to ma honor. Time was, Ah might have killed the impudent rascal for half as much. Time was. Time passes. Time passes. Honor does not, though the passion one feels for it may waste away. Ah felt ma-self past killing for it.

August 1884

Ah should have known better when it came to Billy Allen. Ma judgement was surely fogged by medication, though Ah cannot now recollect if it was whiskey or the opium elixir on that occasion. No matter. Ah found ma-self impecunious and in need of a small loan. Five dollars seemed a trivial amount, and Billy Allen, for all our past troubles, was more than willing to oblige for a promise of repayment within the week. The week passed. Regrettably, Lady Luck turned her back on me once again. Ah found Billy tending bar in the Monarch Saloon.

"Come to pay up, Doc?" He said polishing a glass.

"Regrettably no, Billy. Misfortune besets me. Ah shall need a little more time."

"What the hell you think I am, a bank? Listen here, you stinking drunk, pay me by noon Tuesday or I'm comin' for you and all them dead pards you an' Earp killt."

Ah took ma leave without further incident. When Tuesday arrived, Ah received word Allen was armed and asking around for me.

Ah took the precaution of having ma Colt hidden behind the bar in Hyman's. Unable to repay a five-dollar-loan, the fine for a firearm violation posed prospect of financial ruin. On ma way down to the saloon, Ah explained ma plight to Mannie Hyman and asked him to notify the police Billy Allen was about courting trouble. Ah hoped police protection might avert trouble. Once in the saloon, Ah took a place at the end of the bar within reach of ma weapon.

Billy Allen entered Hyman's with his hand in his pocket in the fashion of concealing a gun. He scanned the room. His gaze came to rest on me. Ah pulled ma pistol and shot him a wounding graze to the arm. Ma second shot narrowly missed killing him as he slumped to the floor. At this, the bartender disarmed me, sparing the miscreant's life.

Ah was promptly arrested and charged with attempted murder. Bail was set at five thousand dollars. It might as well have been five hundred thousand for ma impecunious circumstances. John Morgan, owner of the Board of Trade Saloon, made bail. Consider the irony. Had Ah borrowed five dollars from John to repay Alan's loan, the whole ugly matter might well have been avoided. Pride precluded me from seeking such aid.

Pride. Honor. The code of a southern gentleman. Such things prove a heavy burden amid the vagaries of real life.

Leadville Municipal Courthouse
August 25, 1884

The bailiff strode to the bench. "All rise. Court is now in session, Justice of the Peace William W. Old presiding."

"Be seated. We have before us the People vs. John Henry Holliday to be arraigned on a charge of attempted murder in the shooting of Billy Allen. Attorneys present."

"District Attorney William Kellogg for the prosecution, Your Honor."

"Your Honor, Charles F. Fishback representing the defendant, Judge Milton R. Rice, assisting."

"The bench calls Leadville Police Captain Edmund Bradbury to the stand."

"Do you swear to tell the truth, the whole truth, and nothing but the truth, so help you God?"

"I do."

"Be seated."

Captain Bradbury testified to ma request for police protection from the person of Billy Allen. Frank Lomeister tended bar that afternoon and testified to the same request for a police presence. He also allowed as how killing me would have boosted Allen's notoriety as a gunfighter. Allen's cronies denied he intended any harm to me in coming to Hyman's looking for me.

Ah got ma say over the loan and the threat, the threat having been confirmed by another witness who heard it. Ah told the court Ah saw him with the butt of a pistol in his pocket and shot him. He fell wounded. Ah fired again, for Ah could not have survived him physically on account of ma infirmed condition and the fact he had me bettered by fifty pounds.

Judge Rice offered closing on ma behalf, stressing the threat of violence to ma person, ma requests for police protection, and the physical risk posed by even a wounded Billy Allen. Kellogg, the prosecutor, gave a stem-winder closing in which he declared ma act of self-defense to be no less than murder, premeditated by the placement of a firearm within reach. The prosecutor's accusation in no way supported by the facts of the case or the testimony heard. Justice Old, being a justice of the peace and not a circuit judge, passed the buck. Ah was bound over for trial by jury when the next session of circuit court convened that November.

After twice being continued owing to congested court dockets, Ah finally came to trial the following March with District Judge George Goldthwaite presiding. Witness depositions were read to the jury followed by closing arguments for the prosecution and defense. The jury reached a verdict on the facts of the case, promptly finding me not guilty.

33

Windsor Hotel
Denver
May 1885

Bucking the tiger at Missouri House word reached me. Wyatt Earp was seen checking into the Windsor Hotel. Ah cashed out. Reaching the Windsor lobby, Ah inquired after the desk for Wyatt Earp. As the clerk scanned the register, someone approached ma elbow.

"Doc Holliday, as I live and breathe."

"Wyatt Earp." *Cugh, cugh . . . cugh.* "Wish Ah could say the same."

He apprised me with eyes saying more than words at the appearance of ma condition. Behind him, the statuesque and stunningly beautiful Josephine Marcus gathered all the light in the room around her natural glow. Her dark eyes, too, registered disbelief at ma emaciated frame, though she was too much the lady to say more.

"Ah heard you were in town."

"Just checked in. You remember Josephine."

"Ah do," Ah said with a slight bow. "Ah don't mean to intrude. Ah thought we might have a drink."

"Josephine has been talking about a bath since we had lunch on the train. Now might be the ideal time if you'll excuse two old friends a few moments time."

She smiled. "My pleasure." She kissed Wyatt on the cheek and set off for their room. We watched her go.

"Ah see Ah was right."

"Right?"

"About San Francisco."

"You did say something about that, didn't you?"

"Eighty-two, wasn't it?"

"It was. So, I did."

"Near certain you would."

"That obvious?"

"That obvious."

"Where's the bar?"

"This way."

"I knew you'd know."

"That obvious?"

He laughed.

Ah led. The Windsor Saloon was in tasteful company with the standard of elegance the hotel set for itself and its guests. Polished pegged wood lobby gave way to hushed atmosphere furnished in dark wood, with red velvet upholstery, draperies, and massive mirrored bar lighted by cut crystal chandelier. Ah took us to a corner table and signaled the waiter for a bottle. Wyatt declined as usual and ordered a beer.

"How long do you plan to be in town?"

"Just passing through. We leave for Cheyenne tomorrow, westbound for California."

"San Francisco?"

"Josephine likes it."

"And what Josephine likes, Josephine gets."

"I seem to recall Kate having some sway over you."

"Haven't seen her for some time."

"Likely you will again."

"Likely and seeing people again," — *cugh, cugh . . . cugh* — "don't go together the way they once did."

"That bad?"

"That bad. Had to give up a good run at the tables in Leadville last year. Couldn't take the winter cold up there. Things are a little better down here. More to the air. As things stand, these lungs must breathe twice as hard to get half as much done."

"Sorry to hear that, Doc."

"Ah know, old friend. Nothing to be done for it."

He lifted his chin to the bottle. "Little less of that might help."

"Man's gonna die. Better dulled than not. Now let's not spend this time given to maudlin reflections on matters beyond our control. We have better things to reminisce about."

"We did have some interesting times together."

"And look at us. Here we are. Walked away from all of them."

"We did."

"Any regrets over the way things ended in Tombstone?"

"Lost Morg. Virg is a cripple. Regret all of that. Righted the family honor. No regrets over that. Did it with the help of good friends like you, Doc."

"What friends are for."

"Doesn't always come with killin'."

"Does when its necessary. True friends in for a penny, are in for a pound."

"Spoke like a damned phil-os-ofer."

"Damned is probably the right of it."

"Some of that goes with the territory for men like us."

"Some. So, what are you and Josephine planning to do?"

He shrugged. "Take it a day at a time, I suppose. Find a way to make some money."

Ah laughed.

"What's funny about that?"

"For all the differences in our circumstances, our occupations are the same."

"There you go phil-os-ofyin' again. Hadn't thought of it that way."

"Man in ma condition has occasion to think. The only difference between us is the amount of occupation left to us."

"Well, hell's bells, Doc, none of us is more than a call away from the hereafter."

"Maybe so, but some of us hear those bells louder than others. Those who don't hear them miss out on all the anticipation. Gives a man purchase to think."

"Hadn't thought of it that way."

"Course not. No reason to."

Silence fell across the table. Ah knocked back ma drink and poured another, sensing unsaid words for farewell.

"Doc, it's been good to see you, but I suspect Josephine is waiting."

"Ah'm sure she is. Fine looking woman, Wyatt. Ah wish you both the best."

"And the same for you."

He rose to take ma hand. We shook holding on to the moment before he turned to go. I watched him. Hell of a man. Hell of a friend. He was gone. Ah sat back down, brushing something wet at the corner of one eye. Picked up ma bottle and poured.

Kate. . . .

Hadn't thought much about her for some time. Seeing Wyatt and Josephine together brought her to mind. Wonder if she still has that boardinghouse in Globe. Probably so. Made her a respectable living to hear her tell it. Couldn't picture ma-self in a settled down life such as that. Settled down and life. Too much of the first let the demons catch up with the last of the second.

Hyman's Saloon
Leadville
February 1887

The cold like to collapsed ma lungs . . . *cugh, cugh, cugh* . . . ah. The potbelly stove in the corner fought a losing battle. Words hung misty in kerosene fog. Ah poured another drink.

"Don't sound good, Doc," Manny said.

"Don't feel good, either."

"It's the mountains and the cold. Ain't good for you. I like havin' you around, but no doubt you'd do better someplace warmer."

"You're a good friend, Manny. Come spring I'll do something. Can't bear the thought of traveling this time of year. Just have to take a seat closer to the fire."

Kate . . .

Ma thoughts drifted. Ah wrote.

Dearest Kate,

I hope this finds you well. Surely better than I. I write of plans to seek treatment at the hot springs in Glenwood come spring. You have recommended it to me on more than one occasion. I am now in full appreciation of the wisdom of your advice. I write in hope you will consider joining me. We have enjoyed so many good times. I should like to see if we might find a few more as time permits. Join me if you will. If you do not, I shall understand. I have not been the best of companions to you. For that I am truly sorry. For your part you have been a rock to me when I found myself most in need. I hope you can forgive the times I behaved badly. It was not in any way your doing. It is the curse I carry in my chest where love should be. I hope we have time to make amends.

In all affection,

Doc

34

Glenwood Hotel
Glenwood Springs
May 1887

Kate accepted ma invitation to join me in Glenwood Springs. She arrived in May, unprepared for the state of ma condition. Ah was skin and bone, with a near constant cough and lungs flooded in phlegm and blood. Ah had little appetite and picked at a bowl of soup in the hotel dining room the evening she arrived. Conversation lapsed in and out of awkward silences.

"Doc, darlin', what am I to do with you?"

"Put up with me, for a time," Ah said. It was the closest Ah could come to humor.

She bit her lip in thought. "My brother has a cabin over in Crystal Valley near the Penny Hot Springs. Soaking in them is known to be therapeutic. Perhaps they would help you. Would you be willing to try?"

"If it shall keep you by ma side, Ah shall try anything. At this point there seems little to lose."

"Don't say that, Doc. Not now. We've only just gotten together. Things must be put to right if they can."

Ah did not disabuse her of her hope. "Ah didn't know you had a brother, darlin' "

"I never talked of family much. Running off as I did so young, we lost touch. I only recently came into contact with him."

"Are you sure he would welcome a lunger into his home?"

"He will if I ask. He is married to a lovely woman who will make us more than welcome. I shall see to the arrangements. Now eat some more of that soup. We need to put some meat on your bones. You need your strength."

"It would go down better with whiskey."

"Some things never change." She signaled the waiter.

"They don't, do they." Ah left it at that.

Penny Hot Springs
Crystal Valley
The heat of the hot spring basin warmed ma bones. The steam stank of sulfur. If that was intended to clear ma lungs, Ah could not put a fine point on the effects. The best

part of the treatment may have been Kate joining me in the pool. We sat upon a stone bench immersed side-by-side.

"How are you feeling, Doc?"

"As good as Ah might, considering."

"What is that supposed to mean?"

"What it says. Ah'm all right, considering."

"Considering what?"

"Considering Ah'm a sick man, buoyed by present company and the caring circumstances of ma treatment."

"Something to be said for that I suppose. I'm glad."

"Course living on a diet of fish and vegetables has its limits, and speaking of limits, I believe Ah'm down some in ma whiskey ration."

"All of it for your own good, including the whiskey."

"Man's gonna die sober in misery or dull to the pain."

"Don't say that, Doc. We're trying to make you well."

Ah extended ma arm to her. "Come here, love. Lay your head on this chest and listen to what passes for ma breathing." She came to me. Ma chest rose and fell with the rattle of death. "That there is what drowning sounds like." She squeezed me hard as though she might will life into me. I believe she hoped she could. Been a while since anyone cared for me like that. "That feels better."

By late summer it became clear ma condition would not improve. We bid our thanks and farewells to Kate's brother and sister-in-law. Kate escorted me back to Glenwood Springs, where we took separate rooms.

Glenwood Hotel
Glenwood Springs
October 1887

Kate was an angel of mercy. She supported us, nursing me when she could. Ah passed ma days taking air on the hotel veranda or seated in the hotel lobby. By autumn Ah found Ah needed a good deal more bedrest. These times Ah hovered between twilight sleep and ma thoughts drifting.

Ah saw them once again, gathered on the platform, under a blazing Georgia sun, remnants of a youthful life about to be left behind. Left behind never now to be recaptured for all the illusion covered over the years. Those family years remained good years, until Mother passed. Ah recall the kin come to see me off. Come again to see me off once more. They told me dry climes in the west would restore ma health. They

315

told me. They hoped. Dry climes as Ah have lived them offered no cure to ma disease. Ah doubt they ever offered more than hope. False hope at that. The dreadful disease that took Mother shall claim me too. Ah thought to fight it. In the vigor of youth, Ah believed Ah could. Death rides a pale horse. Relentless the rider comes.

Still, Ah see them there. Father stands hat in hand as he should. Surprised he came at that. Surprised he stood there still. Perhaps a show of some remorse, though Ah doubt it. Henry Burroughs Holliday married a woman scarcely older than Ah. Married young Rachel under a scandalous cloud of suspicion before Mother's bones grew cold in the grave. As a young man, Ah could not remain under the same roof with the odor of adultery fouling the air. It hurts ma chest to laugh, but Ah chuckled. Adultery a foul odor after the life Ah have lived. No matter. Ah loved Mother far too much to tolerate such betrayal. Education took me to Atlanta to Uncle John and Aunt Permelia.

Dr. John Stiles Holliday encouraged ma interest in a career in dentistry. Ah owed him a debt from infancy for seeing to the surgical repair of ma cleft pallet. It was he who gave me ma first pistol, an 1851 Colt — taught me to use it, too. Knowing ma use of the skill he may have had second thoughts as to the wisdom of that, though Ah value it. Saved ma life more than once. Saved it more than once for this . . . *cugh, cugh, cugh.* Aunt Permelia Ellen Ware Holliday. Ah see her standing beside Uncle John. Ah loved her second only to Mother for the kindness and care with which she received me into her home.

Cousin Robert Alexander Holliday stands beside Aunt Permelia. A cousin by kin, in all ways a brother. Inseparable we were. Tall, slim, blond hair, blue eyes, and handsome in those days, we often were taken for brothers. *Cugh, cugh.* That was then, of course. When Robert chose dental school, we planned a joint practice. That was before the horseman came for me. Best laid plans.

Ma gaze next rested on Sophie. Dearest Sophie Walton, a negro slave who nannied the children. She taught us to play the gambling card game she called skinning. Two valuable skills came of those lessons. The game resembled faro, ma tiger and livelihood. Skinning taught me to count cards, playing for matchsticks. Matchsticks then, matchsticks now. Fortune comes to nothing more.

Lastly, Mattie is there for me. Perhaps this time for the happiness we both desired but could never have. Golden curls, eyes so soft Ah might have drowned in them. Skin of porcelain, a voice to soothe a raging soul, and lips to stir it to rage. Mattie dearest one of all. We grew up kindred spirits. Close cousins. In time we grew to love deeply. Scarcely dared admit it to ourselves lest anyone should suspect, though we knew. A love and longing so strong it felt painful. Cousins were known to wed on occasion, but not in the Holliday clan. Tragic love, forbidden by blood and strictures of her Catholic faith. Social mores denied requite to our love, but what remains in our hearts to this very day cannot be denied. We might have had it yet in some next life, though she, having given her heart to God and the life of a nun after joining the Sisters of Mercy, can expect a far more gentle eternity than that in store for me. Ah suspect the rider of the pale horse has a rather different plan for one such as me.

They are all there in the eye of the mind as they were on that railway platform lo these many years ago. Ah see them again, waving farewell.

35

November 8, 1887
9:55 A.M.

Kate knocked lightly at the door carrying the breakfast tray. "Breakfast is served, Doc."

Ma eyes fluttered. Ah could not raise ma head. *Cugh, cugh . . . cugh, ah . . . cugh.* "Not . . . not today, darlin'." Ah barely managed a whisper.

She set the tray on the nightstand and bent her ear to ma lips.

"Not . . . not today, darlin'."

"You must eat, Doc."

Ah managed a weak smile.

"What amuses you?"

"My feet."

"Your feet?"

Ah nodded with ma eyelids. "Always thought Ah'd die with my boots on."

"Take it for a sign. Not today."

"Today? Ah may be fodder for worms."

Ma eyes drifted dark.

"Don't say such things, Doc."

. . .

"Doc. Wake up, Doc."

. . .

"Doc . . . oh, Doc!"

10 A.M.

I had a cry. Not for long. Still, I needed it. For as long as we knew this day was coming, I wasn't ready for it. I don't suppose we are ever ready for a loss like that. We'd had our ups and downs to be sure. Lives we led, who could have expected anything more. For all of it, we had our together all those years. All those years. And now he's up and gone and left me to finish the rest of it. I cried some again, I admit. For me this time. Maybe only for a minute. Things needed doing.

The undertaker, for starters. Doc needed a proper burying. Needed it now with winter coming on. Couldn't abide the thought of him frozen in some icehouse waiting for spring to thaw. Sent the bell boy and waited.

Skinny runt in a black suit, of course. "I'm sorry for your loss."

"Of course."

"How may I be of service?"

320

Really? "I need Doc buried."

"Ground's beginning to freeze. Might need to wait until spring."

"I need him buried today." He shakes his head. Damn it man, today! "Do I need to get my purse?" *That* did it. My reputation around town was well known including the pistol in my purse.

"I'll call my crew. We'll see what we can do."

"See to it, and get it done."

"Who will officiate at the graveside?"

"Graveside?"

"Service."

"Shit, leave it to me."

Graveside service. Doc would want it. His mother raised him Methodist. None of them handy. He'd befriended Father Downey, the local Catholic priest. Likely put up to it by the love of his life, the cousin who was a nun. Never could get over that. Kate Elder, consolation lover to a nun. Inquiry found Father Downey out of town. That settled the service on Doc's other clerical friend, Reverend W.S. Randolph. Presbyterian. Best I could do.

Pallbearers and mourners came next. Can't have a proper funeral without some of them. All I had to do was visit a couple of saloons. Word spread to the sporting crowd. Turned out Doc had a lot of friends.

The undertaker arranged to transport Doc's remains to Linwood Cemetery. I expected a hearse. The trail to Linwood turned out rough and steep. The elegant hearse, with glass viewing drawn by a matched team of black horses bedecked with black plumes on their headstalls, turned out to be a mule drawn wooden sleigh. Ah well, the mourners made a fine procession following my Doc to his final resting place.

Linwood Cemetery
4:00 P.M.

The grave diggers found a plot they could dig following the futility of frozen false starts. I had my purse with me just in case, though it wasn't needed. The grave proved a pretty, peaceful spot for a man to rest overlooking the town below. Of that I approved. As to the cold wind blowing down the mountain, I could only offer thanks to the mourners, many of whom fortified themselves against the cold with bottles and flasks tucked in their coats. A warmth I partook of. Doc would have approved.

Reverend Randolph laid John Henry Holliday to final rest the afternoon of his death. That he knew Doc personally and something of his story gave weight to his words. The Doc he knew was a quiet, gentle man, suffering the effects of tragic illness. He allowed as how Doc was well liked as evidenced by the large number of his friends come to pay their respects. He glossed over the notoriety of Doc's reputation, paying tribute to the man Glenwood Springs knew, a man of warmth and good humor. I thought it a fine way to be remembered, after all we'd done to leave something of another remembrance.

Rest in peace, John Henry Holliday.

AFTERWORD

Kate

Following Doc's death, Kate left Glenwood in search of respectability. She moved to Carbondale, Colorado. Now known as Mary Horony, she met and married mine owner George Cummings. In 1895, the promise of a copper strike drew the couple to Bisbee, Arizona. Mining success George enjoyed in Colorado eluded him in Arizona. They drifted from prospect to disappointment as tension built in the marriage. Kate carried her familiar feeling of wanting to settle down. George yearned for the next strike to the next claim, turning to the bottle when fortune failed him. A recurring theme among Kate's romantic interests. The couple divorced in 1899.

Divorced and alone on the frontier at age forty-nine, Kate, now known as Mary Cummings, found housekeeping work at the Rath Hotel in Cochise Station, Arizona.

There she learned her employer, John Rath, and his wife both had connections to the Tombstone Cowboy faction. Fearing her true identity might be exposed, Kate left soon after, taking a housekeeping position in Dos Cabezas. Fortunate for her, as events would unfold.

In July 1900, Warren Earp was gunned down in Cochise Station by a Cowboy named Boyett. This prompted Virgil Earp to visit Cochise to pay his respects at Warren's grave. He stayed at the Rath Hotel, where he surely would have recognized Kate and exposed her.

In Dos Cabezas, Kate was employed by English-born miner John Howard. Life as a simple domestic agreed with Kate at this stage in her life. She spent twenty years in that quiet life. Howard was divorced and estranged from his twin daughters. Kate served as both companion and friend. When Howard died, Kate administered his estate inheriting most of it, though with the mining boom having run its course, very little of value could be taken from it.

At eighty years old in 1930, Mary Horony, Kate Elder, Mary Cummings was homeless and penniless. She petitioned for admission to the Pioneer Home in Prescott, Arizona, and was admitted in 1931. The Pioneer

Home met the late-in-life needs of more than a few colorful veterans of Arizona's frontier days, among them Indian fighter General George Crook and small-time rancher John Miller, who went to his grave denying he was Billy the Kid. Kate lived at the Pioneer Home until her passing in 1940. She is interred as Mary K. Cummings.

Wyatt & Josephine

Not long after John Ringo met his demise, Wyatt made his way to San Francisco and Josephine Marcus. It is doubtful they waltzed in the snow as idyllically portrayed in the iconic film *Tombstone.* Fog would have been more likely climatically, though not cinematographically idyllic, if even they danced. What we do know is they began a long and faithful relationship, somewhat out of character for both, certainly so for the mercurial Josephine.

Josephine was a young woman born of wealth and privilege which fashioned her taste for the finer things in life. Wyatt aspired to wealth and prominence, though real wealth eluded him the whole of his life. Josephine satisfied herself with Wyatt's hard-scrabble pursuits for more than forty years. Wyatt did achieve some measure of prominence if that can be counted to notoriety.

The gunfight and vendetta ride rendered him a legendary figure, a legend that followed him for the rest of his life.

Wyatt's quest for wealth kept the couple on the move. A saloon in Idaho, followed by financing mining speculations, and real estate investing in San Diego, where he would lose everything. Josephine took him home to San Francisco where Wyatt connected to the local horse racing scene and played the ponies with some success.

San Francisco began a prolonged campaign to burnish Wyatt's reputation and legend in print, beginning in 1896. As was the case with so many high-profile frontier westerners like George Custer, Wild Bill Hickok, Billy the Kid, Buffalo Bill Cody, and Wyatt's friend, Bat Masterson, the line between fact and fiction blurred in fanciful depiction. Fact or fiction, notoriety followed, conferring a certain celebrity to greet dawn of the twentieth century.

A promising run in San Francisco came to a bitter end over a heavyweight title fight Wyatt refereed in 1896. The fight, pitting "Sailor" Tom Sharkey against Bob Fitzsimmons, drew national attention. It got off to a bad start when Wyatt entered the ring carrying a concealed pistol for which he was disarmed and subsequently fined. Later in the fight with Fitzsimmons handily in control, a low blow felled Sharkey. Wyatt saw the blow and disqualified Fitzsimmons. The punch was screened from ringside observers leading the partisan betting fraternity to scream fix. Wyatt's reputation and integrity were sullied nationwide. Bat Masterson, now a sportswriter for a New York daily, covering the fight game, staunchly defended his friend. Bat flatly stated Wyatt Earp would never do such a thing. The fact Sharkey bore a mark from the blow on his body did nothing to silence those charging the fight was fixed. They claimed an iodine injection could be made to fake the mark on Sharkey's body. The aftermath of the Sharkey Fitzsimmons fiasco set Wyatt and Josephine on the road to a new gold strike and Alaska.

The Alaska goldfield produced a profitable saloon for a few years before cold weather called out for warmer climes in Nevada. When the Nevada gold strike failed to materialize, Los Angeles beckoned with a new chapter aimed at cashing in on legacy and legend. Larger than life frontier figures were hot entertainment properties in the early 1900s. "Buffalo Bill" Cody set the standard with wild west extravaganzas featuring the likes of Wild Bill Hickok, Sitting Bull, and Annie Oakley among others. Libbie Custer burnished her husband's life and legend with two highly flattering biographies. Bat Masterson paid tribute to frontier pals, including Wyatt, in a series of magazine stories. Who better to benefit by such public interest than the legendary Wyatt Earp? The problem Wyatt faced was finding a biographer who could write his story in a fashion attractive to a publisher proved as elusive as that never discovered gold strike.

Around this time, Hollywood and Wyatt discovered each other. Hard to say who discovered whom. Wyatt became good friends with western film actor William S. Hart along with director John Ford, a man who would become a western film giant. Both used Wyatt to consult on their films. Hart once tried to convince Wyatt to appear in one of his oaters. Wyatt refused. Hart next tried to convince Bat Masterson, whom he also befriended, thinking Wyatt might agree if Bat came along. Bat, too, declined. Bat may have declined to appear in Hart's film, but both he and Hart agreed Wyatt's life should be done in a book. Bat piqued Stuart Lake's interest in the project.

The Lake project suffered fits and starts. While Wyatt and Josephine liked the idea and hit it off with Lake, the project faced obstacles Lake could not overcome, starting with Wyatt. Always a man of few words, he became more so with age and infirmity. Health issues hit both Wyatt and Lake, delaying the project, until death intervened in January 1929 with Wyatt's passing.

AUTHOR'S NOTE

Researching Doc Holliday's story proved interesting for the variety of perspectives from which it could be seen. As listed in the selected sources that follow, we had a family history, a perspective *According to Kate,* as well as Doc's associations with Wyatt Earp and to a lesser degree Bat Masterson. The events of Doc's life can be viewed from at least two and sometimes three unique perspectives. The family view glosses over some of the seamer sides of Doc's life. Kate has her own view sometimes distorted by her personal animas toward Wyatt and objections to Wyatt's influence on Doc. Some of Kate's perspective may have been influenced by her desire to serve her own respectability and later in life the possibility of faulty recollection. In accounts of Doc's part in Wyatt's life, we looked to reliable historian portrayals. The same is true with Bat Masterson, though he, a man of letters, gives us a more personal confirmation of his feelings for Doc. What emerges is a complex character. A composite we attempt to synthesize.

Doc considers himself a southern gentleman with all the trappings, code of honor, and expectations of propriety that go with it. By upbringing, he is all of that. He is charming and a loyal friend to those he chooses to befriend. He can also be mercurial, temperamental, judgmental, and easily offended. I speculate disease had much to do with that along with the loss of his mother and betrayal by his father. I endeavored to treat him that way in the story.

Characterizing Doc Holliday in a biographical novel is reminiscent of the challenge we took on with young George Patton in *Boots and Saddles: A Call to Glory.* For most readers "George Patton" is George C. Scott's iconic portrayal in the film *Patton.* The younger character had to remain faithful to the icon he would become in the reader's imagination. In taking on Doc Holliday, I confess to having revisited the same device. This time the icon is Val Kilmer's portrayal of Doc in the film classic *Tombstone.* In fact, I could visualize the cast of that film for the Earp brothers, Kurt Russell's Wyatt in particular. If Bat Masterson sounds something of the portrayal in my book *Friends Call Me Bat,* he should.

— Paul Colt

SELECTED SOURCES

Holliday Tanner, Karen, *Doc Holliday A Family Portrait,* University of Oklahoma Press 1940

Enss, Chris, *According to Kate,* Two Dot, 2019

Guinn, Jeff, *The Last Gunfight,* Simon & Schuster Paperbacks, 2012

DeArment, Robert K., *Bat Masterson The Man and the Legend,* University of Oklahoma Press 1925

Clavin, Tom, *Dodge City,* St. Martin's Press, 2017

ABOUT THE AUTHOR

Paul Colt's critically-acclaimed historical fiction crackles with authenticity. His analytical insight, investigative research, and genuine horse sense bring history to life in dramatizations that entertain and inform. Paul's Great Western Detective League series does action-adventure western style. *Grasshoppers in Summer* and *Friends Call Me Bat* are Western Writers of America Spur Award honorees. *Grasshoppers in Summer* received Will Rogers Medallion Award recognition. *Boots and Saddles: A Call to Glory* received the Marilyn Brown Novel Award, presented by Utah Valley University. Reviewers recognize Paul's lively, fast-paced style, complex plots, and touches of humor. Readers say, *"Pick up a Paul Colt book, you can't put it down."*

Paul lives in Wisconsin with his wife and high school sweetheart, Trish. To learn more, visit Facebook @paulcoltauthor.

Printed in the USA
CPSIA information can be obtained
at www.ICGtesting.com
JSHW020945191124
73880JS00001B/30

9 781420 516050